The Path Not Taken

Published by Mary Strickland, 2024

Copyright: Mary Strickland

All rights reserved. No part of this publication may be reproduced or transmitted by any means including electronic, mechanical, photocopying or otherwise, without prior permission of the author.
ISBN: 978-1-7391172-2-1

Design: www.istudio21.co.uk

For Nigel

“

It doesn’t do to dwell on dreams and forget to live

Preface

January 1970
Bonn, Germany
The *Westland Scout* helicopter lurched violently to the right with a screech of metal on metal and then plummeted. There was nothing that Murray could do and the last things that he remembered were the dual sensations of shock and disbelief and the throttle being wrenched from his grasp as they tumbled out of the sky in a shock of white mist.

He learned later that he'd been in a coma for a week after hitting powerlines on the outskirts of the city while his passenger, General Bernard Verney had been killed. Two military aides had also been critically injured, although survived.

A court martial absolved him of blame, but it was the end of his military career and ferocious headaches, mood swings and flashbacks plagued him for months. It was perhaps inevitable that although he was back at work by June, it only lasted for a couple of weeks before he and the Army parted company by mutual agreement.

The guilt was the worst thing. They only cleared him because extensive tests on the battered wreckage had proved inconclusive, but at the end of the day he'd never know for sure. The cables should have registered on his radar, but had he missed the warning or had the equipment malfunctioned in the fog, as the court martial had eventually concluded?

It wasn't in his favour that he was a relatively inexperienced pilot, having only qualified six months earlier after transferring from the 11th Hussars—a splendid cavalry regiment which had sadly amalgamated with the 10th Hussars and exchanged horses for tanks. That hadn't suited Murray at all and hence his transfer to the *Army Air Corps* in Paderhorn, Germany at the grand old age of 29. It already felt like a lifetime ago and moving on was going to be easier said than done.

His six months of training had been uneventful and since then he'd completed nearly 200 trips to bases throughout the northern Rhine region, but in the court of public opinion it was the meagre six months that counted and not the 150 or so trips made during that time, nor the way that he'd known the routes and the controls like the back of his hand.

He knew instinctively what they said behind his back—that it was probably his fault, even though nothing was proved—and he felt *so* angry, all the time at the terrible injustice of it all. They were goons, the lot of them. Invisible, malevolent and intent on destroying him, but he'd bloody well show them that he was cut out for better things.

However, quite what form those better things might take was a conundrum which he didn't resolve until his return to England in July 1970, at which point his father suggested that he take some time out and do a degree. Captain Claude Woodall had never found his youngest son easy and the two had frequently clashed in the past, but he realised immediately that this accident had left Murray even more volatile than previously.

And so it was that 1st Lieutenant Woodall exchanged a career flying helicopters for a BSc in Political Science at the *London School of Economics*.

Chapter 1

Three years later, July 1973
Du Kane Court, Chelsea, SW3
It was fair to say that the last two months hadn't been kind to Murray and it had come as something of a shock, because in other respects the aftermath of his helicopter accident had gone remarkably smoothly. In fact, so smoothly that it was gratifying.

It was studying which had done it, of course, and he'd emerged with a coveted BSc in Political Science not only with first class honours but also with the highest mark in the London area, for which accolade he'd been awarded the princely sum of £150. By any standards the prize had been low profile as the cheque was simply sent to him in the post with a letter of congratulation and after three years out of work there was no doubt that the cash would come in very handy.

He could have invited his father and stepmother to the degree ceremony, but preferred not to have them there. His father had, after all, conspired against him all his life in concealing Murray's true birthright and it almost made him laugh, sometimes, that his 'parents' remained in blissful ignorance of the fact that he'd long ago seen through all the lies and fabrication surrounding his true identity. He could even remember the hypnosis, for God's sake, and he couldn't even begin to imagine how they'd explain *that* away.

It gave Murray a tortured sense of satisfaction to know everything when they thought that he didn't, but still he had a problem.

It was undoubtedly the soothing balm of academia which had kept him sane for the duration of his degree. There was something about the smell of books, the grand halls and the genius which imbued its very walls and furniture which had provided a natural anaesthetic to the thorny issue of real life. And to the *goons*.

Only the mental gymnastics which went with study had enabled Murray to resist the efforts of the goons to infiltrate and disrupt his life and the fact that his degree had come to an end was now a source of huge concern. He'd find another way to outwit them, but what? For now he was at a loss.

Murray could feel them watching and waiting, closing in. But to what purpose? Detection had only become possible over time because he'd developed coping strategies, but even now he knew very little about them except that they were invisible and had been sent by his 'adopted' family to spy on him. However, he was cleverer than all of them put together and they'd never get the better of him.

His father, Claude, had probably scaled down the goons' activities over the last three years in recognition of Murray's splendid brain being focussed on the acquisition of a first-class degree, but in reality he'd never let his guard down. Had those slippery, grey shadows been there he'd have known about it immediately, but they *hadn't* been there and it was only in the last couple of months that he'd become aware of them again: slippery, slimy things which melted into innocuous everyday objects before dissolving like foam. However, they'd at least given him a break for the entire duration of the course, for which he was grateful.

He didn't want to declare war on Claude and had even been willing to call a truce, but the return of the goons was the last straw and he knew that they'd been following him for at least a couple of months now. There'd even been one or more in the grand hallway when he'd emerged from his final exam in May—they really didn't miss a trick and he wondered how on earth his father had managed to time it all so precisely. Perhaps he'd phoned up the college, or how else could he have known exactly when Murray would be there?

It was perhaps fortunate that the goons had no specific physical form which could be re-imagined in his nightmares, because that would have been too much for his tortured mind to bear. As it was, they were featureless, sexless and stupid... but nevertheless they followed him, listened and made a nuisance of themselves. One was even watching him now and he glared angrily at the television, because that was their favourite place to hang out when the contraption was switched off and he could imagine them gathering at *goon socials* to map out their next moves of watching, following, listening and waiting.

During the course, Murray had been feeling so relaxed without them breathing down his neck that he'd even been taking the medication his doctor had prescribed—but it was too dangerous to do that now, because he had to have all his wits about him for 24 hours a day. The enemy was remorseless and merciless, so he needed all his mental faculties fully operational for what was effectively a game of *cat & mouse*.

Mercifully, he'd long ago discovered how to handle them in certain situations. For example, when he was asleep he kept a candle burning next to him because they hated light of all kinds and especially naked flames. However, coming off the medication always disturbed his sleep and on top of that he was also contending with the burning anger which had never really left him.

He sighed and turned the television on, although with the volume off. That would get rid of the bastards for a while.

He felt a lot older than his 32 years—or nearly 33 now. Since leaving the Army he'd let his hair grow for the first time since he was a teenager and was faintly surprised that it hadn't gone grey yet, with all the stress he'd been under. He had thick, wavy brown hair down to his shoulders, blue eyes and high cheekbones which lent weight to a growing conviction that his real origins were aristocratic. According to various relatives he'd been a beautiful child and many of those same physical qualities had translated into adulthood. Partly thanks to years of rigorous Army training his body was lithe and sinewy—primed for fight or flight at any moment—although in a nod to modern trends he'd taken to dressing down.

The casual observer might have imagined that this laid-back image was a knee jerk reaction to 12 years of rigid formality in the Army, but actually Murray had rather enjoyed all that. It suited the madness of his soul to have those things which *were* under his control kept rigorously neat, tidy and formulaic and that applied even to the minimalistic furniture in his flat. In fact, he took this to such lengths that a visiting student from his course at the *London School of Economics* had assumed he'd just been burgled.

But there were other influences in his life now, and from a most unlikely quarter. Against all probability, the torn bellbottom jeans, loud shirts and camouflage jacket which were his new uniform owed much to his favourite TV programme—*Citizen Smith*. It had even become something of an obsession, that half hour comedy show every Tuesday evening about Wolfie, the loveable Communist who stuck two fingers up at just about everything and everyone. That was how Murray felt and he wondered how the relevant governing bodies had missed censoring such a subversive message.

He pondered whether the writers might have lulled their TV bosses into a false sense of security by disguising politics with humour, although in truth some of the 'frothier' elements were hopelessly inane and didn't sit well with Murray's cerebral side. All the same, it was a salve of sorts and a balm to the brain which spent so much of its time on fire.

When he was in the street, Murray *was* Wolfie and the goons could f-off and die. He wondered if they actually *could* die—there was so much about them that he still didn't know, despite their depressingly long mutual acquaintance.

For some time now he'd been considering a showdown with his so-called father, but to what purpose? He'd only deny everything and cast aspersions on Murray's mental state. No, before approaching him he needed to be able to present at least the main facts of his case: exactly who he *was*, for a start, because once he'd found that out, all the cogent details would follow naturally.

He considered bitterly why his real parents might have abandoned him. Could it have been that he was illegitimate? It was a possibility which intrigued and obsessed him, but in the meantime the personas of Wolfie and Communism were a comfort blanket which he pulled over his head every morning along with his *Che Guevara* T-shirt. *They* were his family for now, but at the same time he never forgot about his other family, waiting in the wings somewhere just out of sight until the moment was right for him to claim them.

His thoughts turned to Frank, his Mongol elder brother. They'd bunged him in an institution in Hove, East Sussex in the early 1940s and hardly ever visited him because it was a bit awkward with him never remembering who they were, plus you couldn't get a conversation out of him to save your life. Murray hadn't seen him for several years now—certainly not since he went to Germany and their last meeting had probably been a good two or three years before that. He wondered if he was even still alive, because the family probably wouldn't bother to tell him if he'd died. Soon after Frank's birth the doctors had predicted that he wouldn't live beyond 12, but he'd certainly exceeded those modest expectations and if he was still alive should be about 37 now.

He tried to picture him: overweight, babyish features, dewy blue eyes... garishly dressed by the institution. What a shock it must have been back in 1936 in the gently rolling hills of Hampshire for this mentally handicapped baby to be born to such glamorous and upwardly mobile parents. Of course, Frank may also have been adopted—as Murray had been—although it was extremely unlikely. Murray was the only one of the three who could claim *that*.

And the third sibling was Miriam, in the middle of the two boys. He'd been very close to her throughout their childhood and although only two years older, she'd been like a second mother to him. However, that hadn't stopped her abandoning him in 1960—buggering off to Australia because she wanted to 'see the world'. It was a funny place to choose, too, when Australia had played such a cataclysmic role in their early lives. Well, fuck her. He'd managed just fine on his own, hadn't he?

Murray found himself inexplicably seized by a burning desire to go and find Frank—another innocent victim of this strange, dysfunctional family. It was only about 40 miles or so to the institution in Hove, although it would undoubtedly take him about an hour and a half once he'd struggled through the London traffic. Still, he had nothing else to do and why not make the goons work a bit harder for once?

So far, by *hook or by crook* he'd managed to hold on to the little mustard-coloured *Triumph Herald* which he'd now owned for around four years, having purchased it shortly before his transfer to Germany with the *Air Corps*. It was his pride and joy, yet he could scarcely afford to maintain it now, what with having this £50 mortgage hanging around his neck. He could have moved to a cheaper place, but why the hell should he, when his supposed family was keeping him from his rightful inheritance?

Murray knew intuitively and without a shadow of a doubt that whoever his parents were, they were rich and possibly even titled as well and knowing this was becoming increasingly unbearable as the funds in his own bank account diminished at a rate which corresponded to his absence from the workplace.

The block of flats had private, underground parking and was in a very select part of London. Fashion pioneers *Vivienne Westwood* and *Mary Quant* had really put Chelsea on the map, but Murray had been fortunate enough to buy the flat in 1964, very marginally before the prices had shot up. It was just after he'd left *Sandhurst Royal Military Academy* and taken his first post with the *11th Hussars*. It should have been a job for life and on that basis the acquisition of this modest residence had been a simple one, but so much had happened in the six years since then that those halcyon days seemed worlds away.

He regarded himself critically in the mirror and decided that he looked suitably cool. Wolfie had even taken to wearing eye liner these days, but Murray wasn't quite ready for that yet. Besides, makeup cost money and that was something in short supply at present because all his energies were necessarily ploughed into dealing with the goons. Not for much longer, though, because he'd have to start earning enough money to keep himself afloat.

A journey to Hove would mean putting petrol in the car, but his mind was made up and luckily he had just about enough in reserve to write a cheque.

Chapter 2

It was a fine day and Murray immediately put the hood down, enjoying the sensation of the wind on his face. It was a while since he'd done this because generally he had nowhere to go—or at least, not outside of London. He found a battery-powered torch in the glove compartment and threw it on the back seat. Being such a bright, sunny day he doubted that the goons would try to follow him on this occasion, but the beam of light would be an additional deterrent—notwithstanding that it was effectively invisible in the natural sunshine. He'd built up an arsenal of deterrents over the last few years and was now a master at giving them the slip.

He was familiar with the A-roads leading out of London and headed towards the A23 with confidence, enjoying the warmth of the sun on his face. Eventually Hove was sign-posted and he breathed a sigh of relief that he'd got this far without any disruption from the goons—the torch was evidently doing its job. He'd long since established that mercifully the little critters had no power to move things, or at least not yet. That wasn't to say that they wouldn't learn, though. Where *they* were concerned, one could never take anything for granted.

The Home was called *Marlow Place* and he remembered that it was away from the seafront and in a rather run-down part of town, but although Hove wasn't a particularly big place, it took him a while to locate it, stopping several times to ask. Then finally he saw the familiar, brick-pillared entrance and memories of long-gone days unexpectedly came flooding back to him, from when he and Miriam had first returned from Australia aged 5 and 7, right through to his teenage years. Taken aback, he sat in the small car park with his heart racing and although probably only a couple of minutes passed in that state, it seemed much longer before the chaos diffused and he could think clearly again.

He hadn't seen Frank for around seven years and had never in his life seen him alone. What would they talk about? Would he have to talk to Frank slowly and carefully, as to a child learning to speak? Suddenly Murray wasn't sure if he was up to it, but he'd come all this way now and besides, he couldn't afford to waste the petrol.

Inside the home it was like a big, old house, which was exactly what it once had been—an early 20th century vicarage which had since been extended and now catered for....how many? Murray had no idea, but judging from the high degree of disability of the patients, it probably wasn't very many.

He wandered in through the open front door and as there seemed to be no formal reception, made his way down one of two passageways, drinking in the very 70s patterned carpet of orange and brown swirls which covered what were probably quite nice wooden floorboards underneath. Murray had an instinct born of association that this was the right direction for the dayroom and moved forward cautiously, encouraged by the murmur of voices in the distance.

Then, when he was about half-way down the passage a matronly looking woman in uniform bustled out from the room at the end with her arms full of what looked like washing and he leapt aside as she bulldozed through, ignoring him. So much for common courtesy, he thought huffily, although he'd noticed that as a matter of course, when he was 'Wolfie' people did tend to behave like that. Typical, *bourgeois* prejudice.

He recognised Frank immediately, although he'd put on weight and at 37 years old was already going to seed. He felt a sharp and unexpected dart of empathy—they might not be related by blood, but both had suffered isolation, relegation and neglect from the same stable.

Frank was sprawled clumsily on the floor, a child's wooden jigsaw in front of him. There were probably only about 20 pieces altogether, but the task was evidently perplexing him and some pieces had already been incorrectly forced together.

'Hello Frank. I'm Murray,' he said, staring down at him as if from a great height.

Frank looked up. 'I don't know Murray,' he said, without embarrassment.

'I'm your brother, but I haven't seen you for a long time.' Murray bent down and sat on the floor, so that the puzzle was between them. He noticed that there were five other residents in the room, two of them in wheelchairs and apparently asleep, two more watching a western on television judging by the gunfire emanating from that direction and another seated in a window alcove, staring out over the back garden. They could all have been aged anything between 20-50, but there were no other Mongols like Frank.

'I'm sorry I haven't seen you for so long, Frank, but I had an accident.'

Frank seemed interested for the first time. 'Did it hurt?'

Murray smiled. 'Yes, quite a lot. I was in a helicopter which fell out of the sky.'

Frank's expression was blank. 'What's a helicopter?'

'Something that flies in the air, like an aeroplane or a bird.'

'I like birds.'

Murray didn't reply, but carefully removed one of the incorrect pieces of the puzzle and replaced it with the correct one. It dawned on him that this was a picture of *Noddy* and *Big Ears*, sitting in Noddy's yellow car.

'I've got a car a bit like that,' he said, looking up from the puzzle to see if Frank registered any interest in this fact and was gratified to discover that the effect was electric.

'A *yellow* car!?'

'Yes.'

'My favourite colour is yellow!' Frank's face glowed with an excitement which Murray could scarcely have predicted and for a moment he see-sawed between the conflicting urges of maintaining his customary reserve and responding in kind.

'Can I see it?'

'Of course, but later.' Murray felt instinctively cautious. He wasn't at all sure if he wanted to be responsible for Frank outside of the building and seeing the car would inevitably entail having a ride in it. But it was too late.

'Please, I want to see it.'

'After we finish the puzzle then.' Murray disentangled another couple of pieces which had been wedged together against all the laws of physics and over a period of ten minutes, sat cross-legged on the floor, pointing Frank in the right direction. He quickly learned that the concepts of left and right were best abandoned when it came to giving directions, but eventually both characters sat resplendent in Noddy's flash, open-top cabriolet.

'Now?' asked Frank, barely even registering that the puzzle was completed, and Murray nodded resignedly. He was *Citizen Smith*, for Christ's sake and he didn't need permission to take his own brother out.

Together they walked back the way Murray had come and as they passed through the hallway he thought he could hear the clattering of pans coming from a room at the end of the other passageway. That must be the kitchen, then.

There were only two cars in the car park and only one of them was yellow, so Frank had no trouble in making his way straight there, whereupon he stared at it as if in amazement, stroked the front passenger wing and then bent down to kiss it repeatedly, tears of happiness streaming down his face.

Murray stood in some consternation, not knowing what to say or whether to say anything at all and in the end he simply stepped back and let Frank savour the moment. For the first time he noticed that his brother was wearing a child's yellow T-shirt with a picture of a bulldozer on it, printed in black. Apart from that he was dressed in shapeless, green jogging bottoms and dirty white plimsolls.

He was never quite sure how it happened, but the next moment they were in the car and he was driving them towards the sea front, with the sun beating down and Frank squealing with joy in the passenger seat. Had he not been required to keep at least one hand on the steering wheel, Murray would have covered his ears, because the collective volume of the engine, the wind and the uncensored approbation of Frank was quite overpowering.

At the first opportunity he parked the car on the sea front and beckoned to Frank to get out of the car, which he did somewhat reluctantly, continuing to stroke the shiny bodywork once he was on the outside. Partly to distract him, Murray pointed at the sea just 50 yards away and said, 'Look at that, Frank!'

It seemed to do the trick, because Frank looked horrified. 'What's that?'

It was Murray's turn to be shocked. 'It's the sea, Frank. Haven't you been here before?'

'No. What is it?'

'Just a lot of water, like having a really big bath.' Unaccountably Murray felt tears pricking his eyes. Frank had lived here for over 30 years, just five minutes from the beach and yet no one had ever taken him to the seaside.

'Has anyone ever taken you out of the place where you live, Frank?' he asked, but then remembered that his brother probably only had a very short-term memory. All the same, it really did seem to be the case that he'd never seen the sea before.

'Shall we go down, then?'

Frank looked uncertain. 'Does it hurt?'

'No of course not. Look, you wait here and I'll show you.'

He carefully negotiated the pebbles which led down to the sea, kicked off his shoes and socks and paddled for a few seconds before walking back up the beach to collect Frank, who wasn't looking entirely convinced. However, he sat down about ten feet from the water while Murray resumed his paddling.

After a little while he got to his feet and came to join him, Murray only realising too late that he'd made no attempt to remove his socks and plimsolls first.

'Damn!' he exploded, without thinking.

Frank looked scared. 'Am I doing it wrong?' he asked, and his eyes filled with tears.

Murray almost cried himself. 'No Frank, I just remembered something which I forgot to do this morning,' he excused himself, before asking, 'Do you like the sea, then?'

'Yes, it's nice. Shall we have a bath now?'

Murray could see things getting out of hand and quickly nipped that idea in the bud. 'Next time I'll bring something for you to wear in the water, Frank, but you mustn't get your clothes wet now.'

Frank pointed towards his shoes and socks. 'They're wet.'

'Yes, but it's all right. I'll give you some dry ones to go back to *Marlow Place*.' Murray cast a glance at Frank's shoes and hoped that they took more or less the same size as the only thing he could do was to swap with him.

Frank became a convert to the sea in a very short time and as it was becoming increasingly difficult to prevent him from wading in beyond the depth appropriate for paddling, Murray suggested that they go for a walk instead, in anticipation of which he spent ten minutes doing his best to pull his own dry socks onto his brother's wet feet. Fortunately they were more or less the same size, but Frank complicated his efforts by rolling around on the beach like a playful kitten, to the point that Murray was quite exhausted by the end of it. Fortunately, they were his oldest plimsolls and wouldn't be greatly missed—the socks ditto.

Holding hands, they walked along the sea front, stopping numerous times to admire the brightly coloured pink and white Brighton rock in multifarious designs along with plastic beach shoes, seaside postcards, plastic buckets and spades and...flip flops. It seemed a good idea to buy some flip flops, lest Murray do himself an injury travelling barefoot and he bought a pair of yellow ones, to Frank's delight.

'I'll buy you a pair *next* time,' he promised disingenuously, but then to make up for this disappointment he bought a bucket and spade and somewhat against the odds they managed to find a small, sandy patch on the beach where Frank busied himself in doomed attempts to make the perfect castle. The scenario of him endlessly ploughing on despite repeated failures reminded Murray of Boxer—the carthorse in George Orwell's *Animal Farm*—who never lost faith despite repeated disappointment and receding odds. Personally, he was convinced that those bucket manufacturers designed them precisely so that there was always one corner missing.

Finally, hunger drove them back to the promenade and he bought a large packet of takeaway chips which they shared on the beach, spreading out the newspaper in front of them and weighing it down with pebbles against a backdrop of fierce gusts of wind.

Afterwards, Murray demonstrated the art of skimming flat pebbles into the sea by throwing them so that the smooth surface hit the water, causing them to bounce anything up to three times and Frank stared in wonderment. He tried to master the technique, but his attempts flopped clumsily just a few feet away with a tell-tale plop and he frowned in frustration.

'Next time you can practice more, but we have to go back now,' Murray insisted eventually, suddenly aware that it was nearly 4 pm and that they might be in quite a lot of trouble as a result of their all-day jaunt.

Frank complied wordlessly and instinctively extended his hand for Murray to grasp as they turned to re-trace their steps.

'You do know that I'm your brother, don't you?' Murray asked suddenly, still unsure of how aware this stranger was of absolutely anything except the physicality of here and now. He looked hard at Frank as he spoke and saw a frown of incomprehension cross his brow.

'I mean, we have the same mother and father,' he continued, slightly hysterically, uncomfortably aware than in an attempt to explain the concept, he was lying to Frank in any case, because they *didn't* have the same parents at all. That had always been the big lie.

'I don't know who my mother is,' Frank said slowly, before adding, 'I'm tired. I want to sit down,' and his eyes filled with tears.

With an acquiescence which surprised even himself, Murray immediately sat down on the pebbled ridge which marked the surge of the last high-tide. Normally he felt irritated and even angry at the slightest infringement on his own wishes, but for reasons he couldn't yet fathom, it wasn't like that with Frank.

Of course, Frank wouldn't know his mother. How could he when he'd been cast away from the rest of the family at three years old, when they'd left the country without him before he could even talk.

'Do you want me to tell you about your mother, Frank?' he asked, astonished by the transition which was causing him to care about any person other than himself.

'*Our* mother, you mean,' Frank corrected, taking him by surprise.

'Yes, yes,' Murray muttered, slightly irritated. How was it that his brother could be so utterly childlike and simplistic in some things and annoyingly on-the-ball in others?'

Frank's eyes were shining with excitement now, the transition from tears to joy almost seamless.

Murray hesitated. Where to begin and how much to tell him? And would he even understand or remember? But then he realised that it didn't really matter, because Frank lived for *now* and if he didn't remember, well then, he could simply be told it all again and again if necessary and perhaps some of it would sink in eventually.

'There were three of us children and you were the eldest...' he began.

'My mother, I just want to know about my mother,' Frank interrupted rudely and it was Murray's turn to frown, although in an instant he accepted the reproof. After all, it would make his job easier.

'Her name was Grace and she was very, very beautiful. And she was also very musical and could sing and play the piano beautifully, so she was very popular at dinner parties. And besides all that, she loved drama—you know, acting on stage and all that.' Murray paused, aware that he had to keep his vocabulary simple if Frank was to follow what he was saying.

'You mean like on television?!' Frank's face lit up expectantly.

'A bit like that.'

'Was she a film star?'

Murray began to feel rather emotional himself. He was only speaking from hearsay anyway, because he had himself been only been two years old when she'd died and if truth be told, he couldn't remember her at all. 'She was like a film star to everyone who knew her,' he said, carefully.

'Why did she leave me?' Frank asked, tears suddenly falling down his cheeks and instinctively Murray grasped his hand.

'She didn't want to, she really didn't, it was just the War,' he said, feeling his own eyes fill with tears in a show of empathy which astounded him. 'When the War came, Daddy had to go away to fight in another country because he was in the Army and they sent his family with him, but so that Granny wouldn't be lonely, they left you with her because she needed you.'

'But I don't know Granny. Who is Granny?' Frank asked, puzzled.

'She was Daddy's mummy.'

'But where is she?'

'She died a long time ago,' said Murray. He wondered if he'd ever tell Frank the whole story, about how he'd only been with Granny for just a few short weeks before he'd been sent to live in the home. There may even have been several homes—he wasn't sure of all the details and had only met Frank for the first time a year or so after the War finished, when they'd been about six and ten years old respectively. He certainly couldn't remember their first meeting and hadn't even begun to register those very infrequent occasions until he was a teenager.

He felt that he'd probably said enough for now. 'You've got *me*, Frank, and I'll come and see you often, now that I know where you are. I promise I will, and I'll tell you all about your family.'

He clambered to his feet and pulled on Frank's arm. 'Come on.'

'But I'm tired,' Frank countered, suddenly stubborn.

'If you're good and do what I ask you to do, then I'll tell you the rest of the story next time,' Murray cajoled.

'Do you promise?'

'Yes, I really promise.' Murray felt inexplicably humbled by Frank's blind trust and also rather confused, because recounting even that small fragment of their past had unexpectedly struck a chord within himself.

In truth he had no idea how Grace and Claude had felt about their Mongol son. Even today, mental handicap was taboo, so what on earth must it have been like in 1936 when Frank was born? And with Grace being so beautiful and talented and Claude a rising star in the *Royal Artillery*, to have produced a child with such a serious handicap must have been almost incomprehensible. A shock? A humiliation? Almost certainly both of those things.

He could see why they hadn't felt able to take him to Singapore in 1939. What with the uncertainty of their own future and movements, not to mention local attitudes to mental handicap which were bad enough in England, let alone in the Far East. But what had happened *after* the War was more difficult to explain away.

The walk back seemed very long and he felt exhausted himself by the time they reached the little Triumph Herald, small but perfectly formed and waiting patiently where they'd left it. With a sigh he sank into the driver's seat and leaned over to push the passenger door open for Frank.

'Can I drive?' Frank asked.

Murray laughed. 'Not this time, because I'm in a hurry.'

'I can drive fast.'

'Goodness, look at that enormous lorry blocking the road!' exclaimed Murray instinctively, for the first time in his life acquiring the art of distraction.

In fact, the enormous lorry held them up for another five minutes while it reversed into a surprisingly narrow lane which opened onto the seafront and it gave Murray time to resign himself to some sort of scene once they arrived back at *Marlow Place*. What if the Police were out searching for them? It made him wish for this delay to be as long as possible, to ward off the inevitable uproar that would inevitably greet them and he was almost disappointed when the holdup was over relatively quickly.

Frank was quiet now and they didn't talk on the way back. Murray wondered what was going through his head, if anything.

With a sense of foreboding he drew up in the gravel car park and was relieved to see that although there were a few vehicles there, none of them appeared to belong to the local Constabulary.

Taking Frank's hand, he led him back through the open front door with a sense of trepidation and then through the hallway and was just turning into the passageway towards the *Day Room* when a voice behind them made him jump.

'Well, it's Frank, isn't it?'

It was a member of staff, judging by the unform, but she didn't seem concerned.

'Hello, Daisy,' said Frank, unperturbed.

'We wondered where you'd gone. You know you missed lunch!' she said, only a touch reprovingly.

'I'm his brother. We went for a walk,' Murray explained.

'Oh, well that's all right then,' said Daisy unconcernedly before turning to Frank with the words, 'It's your favourite programme in a minute, if you hurry.'

Frank beamed. 'You mean *The Wacky Races*?'

Daisy nodded and raised her eyebrows in Murray's direction.

It was all turning out far better than Murray could ever have hoped. 'I'll leave you here, then, and I'll come back soon,' he called out to Frank's retreating back, but his brother was already half-way down the passage and for now, at least, it was a case of *out of sight, out of mind*.

He turned back to Daisy. 'Is there a book or anything I should sign if I take him out again?'

She looked thoughtful. 'We should *really* have something like that, but if you just tell someone it should be all right. We wouldn't normally worry unless he wasn't back before dark.'

Murray thanked her and repeated that he'd be back again soon, aware as he did so that it was also a reminder to himself that something unexpected had happened today and that he wanted Frank back in his life. In fact, it was the only member of his 'family' that he did want, and not as a sideshow but as something meaningful. They might not be blood brothers, but he felt closer to him than he had done to anyone for a very long time.

Chapter 3

Clifftops, Sheringham, Norfolk
December 23rd, 1973

Murray sank back on the sofa and looked about him warily. It was one of those old, capacious styles of furniture that tended to swallow anyone daring enough to lean back even slightly and just now he wished that he'd insisted on a hard-backed kitchen chair which would have enabled him to be alert and on his guard.

At the moment there was only Aunt Marjorie and Uncle Roland to contend with, although his cousin Tristan and wife Kathleen were relatively close at hand in the kitchen—slaving over a hot stove, apparently.

Aunt Marjorie was his late mother's elder sister and he had to admit that she looked all right for her age, which must now be late 60s. Judging by photographs of the sisters when they were young, she'd never been anywhere near as good looking as Grace and today her figure was really rather stodgy, but she still had a fine head of coiffured, swept back, dark brown hair and generally made the best of herself with face powder and good taste. She also had a warm personality which tended to draw people to her, not that Murray didn't see right through all *that* artifice.

Roland was tall, stooping and dignified as one might expect from an ex-Army Colonel, but 20 or so years of civilian life had rounded his rough edges and he was apparently quite popular among the residents of the old people's home which kept him solvent. Greying, craggy and with a meticulous eye for detail, he was a good foil to his wife's impulsive good nature.

Murray's father, Claude, had been best friends with Roland when they were both in the Royal Artillery and it was a family joke that after Marjorie had got engaged to Roland in 1930, her younger sister had been so worried about being left on the shelf that she'd snapped up and married Claude within a year of meeting him.

The story went that Grace had previously been in love with a married man and when he refused her ultimatum to leave his wife, she'd married Claude on the rebound. Naturally, this information had never been imparted willingly, but was rather the spoils of eavesdropping when Murray and his sister Miriam were very young.

It had been August 1945 and they'd only recently returned from Australia, where they'd spent most of the War. With their mother dead and their father still in pieces after more than three years in *Changi Jail* as a prisoner of the

Japanese, they'd been sent back on the boat alone in the care of another passenger and their first port of call had been Aunt Marjorie in this very house. It was at that point that he and Miriam had learned the intriguing information about their mother's past and to this day his aunt and uncle had no idea that they'd been overheard—or at least, not that Murray was aware.

They'd crept down from their bedroom one evening when they were meant to be in bed and hidden in the dining room behind an enormous, old, leather armchair. All these years later it was in exactly the same position in the corner of the room and still had the same cream cushion with an abstract pattern in red embroidery. The main gist of the conversation had been less about the past and more that despite Grace's death being tragic, the marriage would never have lasted and at least Claude was now free to marry again and provide a home for the children—by which they meant Miriam and Murray. Noone had ever mentioned Frank.

It gave Murray a start when he suddenly sensed a movement at that very moment and glimpsed the tail end of a goon slithering over the headrest of that same big, old armchair from behind and melting into the fabric. He stared, fixated, but was so deeply sunk into the sofa that his reaction was limited entirely to facial expression.

'Well done for getting that degree, darling, you must be *terribly* proud,' Aunt Marjorie volunteered, a touch tremulously Murray thought, and he was glad that she seemed nervous. They obviously recognised that he wasn't just some thicko that they could push around from pillar to post.

When he didn't immediately respond to his aunt's congratulatory conversation opener, Roland helpfully filled the gap with a reminder about the additional glory of Murray's outstanding grade and corresponding cheque. 'Wonderful achievement after that awful accident,' he chimed in, before adding as an afterthought, 'Do you miss the Army at all?'

For a long time Murray hadn't even given the Army a second thought. 'Not really. I only joined the *Air Corps* because the *11th Hussars* ceased to be a cavalry regiment.'

He purposely didn't elaborate, but Roland affected not to notice. 'Yes, I've a feeling that the Army is a very different institution now to what it was when we went *into* the War. As you know, your father only lasted a couple of years after he came back before deciding that it was time to get out. Didn't agree with the way things were being run, I believe, and it was the same for me. We more or less joined and left together.'

It would have been polite to enter into a discussion about exactly what *had* gone on in the Army after the war, but Murray couldn't be bothered. For a couple of years his father had worked in the *Army Reserves* repatriating Poles and then gone into market gardening, while at around the same time Roland had taken over an old people's home and both had met with reasonable success in their new careers. However, all that hardly seemed important now.

As if reading his mind, Marjorie tried again with another observation. 'I hear your father's thinking of taking over a small holding and going into dairy farming.'

Was he? That was the first Murray knew of it, although it had to be said that he and his supposed father weren't at all close and he couldn't even remember the last time that they'd been in touch. Rather impatiently he knocked back the rest of his sherry and said simply, 'I wouldn't know. He never tells me anything.'

Marjorie looked rather crestfallen and he wondered if she was thinking that she wasn't supposed to have mentioned it. He wouldn't have put it past his father to tell everyone to keep him in the dark—not that he cared.

'He's seen something a few miles away and is trying to raise the money. I think he wants to get his cousin involved in some sort of partnership...' Marjorie tailed off.

Oh yes, that would be it. His rich, spinster cousin whose nickname of *Old Barn* was so ubiquitous that Murray didn't even know her real name, but she rattled around in a large, old, Gothic manor house near Salisbury and had reportedly made her money on shrewd management of an initially modest quota of stocks and shares. The word was that during the War she'd worked with Alan Turing at Bletchley Park on cracking the *Enigma Code* and she was certainly extremely clever.

'It's only 30 acres or so. I think he's hoping to buy a herd of Jersey cows, or rather, not an entire herd, but to build up his own from different cows all over the country. I think the plan is to sell the milk locally and later on move into making butter, if it all goes well...'

Her voice tailed off again in the face of Murray's evident disinterest, but he barely noticed, all his attention now being focussed on what he could make out of the goon which had now moved onto the floor behind the old chair in the exact same space that he and Miriam had once crouched, all those years ago. However, they never stayed still for long and this one now seemed to be melting into the folds of the adjacent floor-length curtain and moving fluidly around it like some sort of binding cord. They always found ingenious ways of moving—sometimes as shadows and sometimes by infiltrating moving objects and even animals.

On the last occasion that he'd visited his father—more than three years ago now—a particularly outrageous goon had possessed a Persian carpet and danced before him in the guise of all the elements of the symmetrical design. Murray had really lost his cool at that point and accused his father of all manner of abuses and crimes, this being the main reason that they'd been out of contact for so long.

'Tell us about your new job—it sounds frightfully exciting,' said Aunt Marjorie, evidently in this for the long haul.

He dragged his attention back towards her. The goon was quiet now, although still alert and listening, but then again, Murray had nothing to hide.

'I'm working for a motorbike courier firm, travelling between London banks,' he told her, matter-of-factly.

'Goodness, I can't imagine how you find your way around!' she exclaimed, affecting brightness. 'I'm hopeless in London and as for having any sort of respectable sense of direction...Well, I'm sure a 5-year-old could manage better.

Murray didn't doubt it for a moment and said nothing to contradict her, whereupon Roland asked, 'Don't you ever get lost? I mean, doesn't it take London taxi drivers months—even years—of study before they make the grade?'

'I only have to do a route once in order to remember it,' Murray declared, with finality.

'I hope they're paying you well, because the pay-off from the Army won't last for ever,' said Marjorie, rather rashly entering unchartered territory.

He fixed her with a stony glare. 'How do you even know about that?' he asked, nevertheless aware that of course his business would have been common gossip within the family and probably outside of it too, for all he knew.

She looked confused. 'Well, only because there always *is* something when one leaves the Army, isn't there? And especially so after an accident.' She hesitated and Murray noticed Roland take her hand, reassuringly. It annoyed him—they were both so pathetic.

'The pay's fine,' he said. It was true. He could keep his *Triumph Herald* at least for now and even had use of the courier company's motorbike for the duration of his job there. In fact, it was an ideal situation for him because he frequently worked early or late, leaving him a lot of free time during the day in which to see Frank. Moreover, the long summer evenings were when the goons became most active and if he could be out working during that time, so much the better. Not to mention that filling his evenings with work helped him to forget that he didn't have a social life.

He was on the point of mentioning Frank when he stopped himself. If it was known that Murray had made his acquaintance and was visiting regularly, they were sure to try and interfere.

At that moment Tristan entered the room and waved a dish cloth absently. 'We're just about ready now, if you want to come through. He was dark haired—standard short back and sides—and of average height and build, but his face was pale and drawn, detracting from what would otherwise have been considerable good looks. Murray knew that he'd had some sort of breakdown because he'd kept in touch to some extent with Tristan's sister Evie and she'd told him about it in a letter.

It was something to do with the collapse of his business making wooden toys and he wasn't quite sure what the current situation was, but in the meantime Kathleen's wage had kept them going. However, with two small children it had all been rather fraught.

Luckily the two little girls had been farmed out to their other grandparents and so weren't here today—much to Murray's relief, because he didn't really like children and certainly didn't feel up to coping with noisy infants. Children of that age were so intrusive and selfish that even the goons didn't like them and as far as he was concerned, that was their only advantage.

Bemusedly he considered the advantages of hiring children for goon duty, but then it was hardly a practical solution because quite apart from the logistical impossibility of acquiring children for the task, they would undoubtedly be far more trouble than the goons.

There was a short period of shuffling around the table while everybody decided where to sit and then finally Murray found himself seated at one end of the six-foot dining table with Tristan and Kathleen on either side of him and Marjorie as far away as possible at the other end, next to Roland who was making himself useful carving the roast chicken.

This dining room was very familiar to Murray, who had been here countless times as a child and teenager. There was the signature old Grandfather clock in one corner—18th century dark oak and intricately carved at a later date—and those two fascinating, early, framed prints of the execution warrants of Mary Queen of Scots and Charles I. Not the typical accompaniment that one might expect to a hearty meal, but they'd always been there, next to the Stubbs-style oil painting of a horse in its stable, painted by some relative of Roland's. And then there was the huge, 18th century, silver tea urn and accompanying platters and jugs which stood on the dark oak sideboard along one wall—yet more family heirlooms.

Roland handed out plates bearing generous portions of roast chicken and they helped themselves to an array of potatoes, carrots and beans which were passed around the table, the conversation initially centring on nothing more innocuous than the food. Then, as the plates gradually filled up and everyone tucked in, Marjorie opened with, 'Murray's just bought himself a piano, Tristan.'

Murray started. It wasn't something that *he'd* mentioned, although he'd told Evie in a letter, so word had obviously travelled that way.

Tristan's drawn expression relaxed slightly. 'You lucky thing, old boy. I've been after one for ages now, but they've all been either too knackered or too expensive.'

Murray savoured the taste of the chicken and bread sauce, which seemed to melt in his mouth. 'How much do you want to pay?' he asked.

'Not more than £50. You probably know that the business hasn't been going well lately, so I can't push the boat out. I'm looking for something second hand, of course, but good quality. Maybe even something that I can restore.'

Marjorie sighed. 'Poor Triss had a bit of bad luck recently when he missed out on a marvellous one which he could have had for £40, but he recognised that it was worth much more than that, arranged for it to be valued and *Harrods* ended up buying it for £400!'

Murray regarded Tristan in astonishment. 'What a fool. It doesn't pay to be generous in this world,' he chided, rather callously.

Tristan blanched but said nothing and Roland answered curtly, 'It was purely a matter of honesty and we're very proud that Triss did the right thing. The owner was naturally extremely grateful to him.'

'I'll bet he was! And did he also give Triss a share of the spoils?' Murray did nothing to keep the sarcasm out of his voice and in the pregnant pause which followed, answered his own question. 'No, I thought not.'

A pink flush crept up Marjorie's chest towards her neck, but both she and Roland remained tight-lipped and only Kathleen appeared not to have taken offence, for she broke the ensuing silence with a placatory remark which gave no indication of being forced. 'I'm sure the right one will come along. We just have to be patient.'

She was a tall, well-built girl with shoulder length, dark hair and blue eyes. By all accounts she'd been quite sporty in her youth and motherhood hadn't yet deprived her of a very good figure. Murray thought he might even have fancied her himself at one time, but his libido had taken rather a hit lately. He couldn't say why, exactly, but that whole scene really didn't interest him and the idea of sharing his life with anyone at all was positively repellent. Having the goons around was bad enough, but actually living with someone who required his attention was unthinkable.

He'd had girlfriends in the past, like all the chaps, but it wasn't an exercise that he felt like repeating in this phase of his life and he hadn't been involved with anyone for at least four years now.

Suddenly Tristan said, 'I hear you've got a flatmate.'

Murray wondered if Evie had actually sent his letter round to the whole family.

'She's a third year LSE student studying political science—the same degree I did,' he volunteered, rather grudgingly, knowing that the news he was sharing his flat with a girl would be received with some incredulity, even though he'd been at pains to point out to Evie that it was *purely* a flat share arrangement and they weren't *living together* as such. This was pretty common in London these days, but he knew that out in the provinces it was still considered very shocking, and particularly to Marjorie and Roland's generation.

'What's she like?' Kathleen asked, boldly. 'I mean, obviously you must get on all right.'

'We don't see each other very much and we barely speak even when we do. It's purely a financial arrangement,' Murray insisted, determined to nip any speculation in the bud.

'Did you make any friends on your course?' Roland persisted, conversationally.

'Some of them were all right and we collaborated on projects occasionally, but I prefer working alone whenever possible and I like my own space, so those relationships didn't extend beyond the course.'

Murray was acutely aware that he wasn't being either forthcoming or cooperative, but he didn't care. They had no right to know all his business and he wished that they'd stop asking questions and talk to each other instead—which in fact was what happened for the rest of the meal, although he didn't take any interest until Tristan mentioned that he'd received £50 from *Old Barn* for Christmas—a gift which had fortunately also been received by Murray.

Old Barn always came up trumps at Christmas, although she wisely ignored birthdays.

'That's something to put towards your new piano at any rate, old man,' Murray suggested, almost pleasantly.

'I'm not sure about that. There are too many other things we need, not to mention the overdue bills which are lining up,' said Tristan, rather sadly.

'You know, you should never have got married,' Murray upbraided him, simultaneously helping himself to the last of the roast potatoes. 'If you hadn't, then you wouldn't have all these other claims on your time and money.'

A shocked silence greeted this statement, broken only by the ticking of the Grandfather clock and the clinking of cutlery on china as the small company homed in on the food as their only distraction, until eventually Tristan said evenly, 'I'm sure that's not a problem *you'll* be having any time soon,' Murray.

'Why not?' he asked, although he thought that actually it would have been more realistic to reply, 'You can say that again!'

'Because she'd have to be an idiot or a Saint to put up with you,' Kathleen responded, dryly.

Murray realised that he was probably meant to be offended by that remark, but he really couldn't be bothered. 'Well, only an idiot or a Saint would get married in the first place,' he shot back, adding after a moment, 'And as I'm neither, you're right, Tristan—it's not a problem I'll be having and meanwhile I can afford a piano and you can't.'

The goon from the drawing room curtain had now followed him through to the dining room and extended itself along the length of the Grandfather clock. He couldn't see it physically, but didn't need to in order to know that it was there and could picture it in his mind's eye: nearly but not quite transparent and at that very moment sinking into the deep grooves of the decoratively carved wood.

Involuntarily he slammed his fist down on the table in frustration and exclaimed, 'Damn and blast this fucking country!' And then watched with some satisfaction as the luncheon party collectively choked, coughed or in Aunt Marjorie's case, scuttled out of the room in alarm, still clutching her knife and fork.

Chapter 4

January 1974

Things had improved a little after that tumultuous lunch with his aunt and uncle in Sheringham. Enough, in fact, for Murray to stick to their original arrangement of staying until December 27th, although it had been touch and go for a few hours and wasn't the first choice of any of the parties concerned. For his part, Murray stayed on only for the food, although subsequently he'd also received some quite nice presents on *Christmas Day*—credit where credit was due in that respect. It had never occurred to him that any reciprocal arrangement might have been expected, but as nobody seemed to have been expecting any gifts from him in any case, no harm was done.

It was also opportune that after the first two days Tristan and Kathleen left, to be replaced by Evie and her husband Gilbert, so it had been a bit like starting all over again, rather than trying to negotiate the detritus of eggshells already crushed and scattered. Luckily his aunt and uncle had kept largely out of his way and that had also helped. He never went out of his way to offend them, but when their paths *did* cross, somehow they always seemed to bring out the worst in him.

At one point he'd tried to talk to them about what he felt, but his aunt had accused him of harking back to the past and then added insult to injury by rubbing in the fact that his sister Miriam *never* did that. The upshot was that Murray decided she and Roland deserved all they got from him, especially as they were almost certainly in on the whole deception in any case—specifically the mystery of his true identity and the dispatch of the goons to spy on him. *They* definitely didn't deserve his goodwill, although he did feel that perhaps he'd been a little hard on his cousins and their spouses. After all, they'd just been children when it was all happening, so it wasn't their fault.

He wouldn't have said that he *liked* his cousins exactly, but they were the only 'family' he had, except for Miriam and she wasn't any good to him out in Australia. She'd been gone since 1960 when she was 21 years old and he'd been at Sandhurst at the time, too preoccupied with his own life to realise what a huge mistake she was making and accordingly had failed to dissuade her from making the greatest mistake of her life.

Besides, at the time she'd said it was only for two years—probably just a placatory carrot to keep everybody quiet—and then at the end of that time had announced that she was staying, by which time it was all a *fait acomplit.*

From the beginning their correspondence had taken the form of tapes rather than letters, the idea being that with so much distance between them, this would be a more intimate means of communication, although it rather backfired when the tapes hailing from his side of the Atlantic became increasingly antagonistic and accusatory. Murray hadn't held back one jot on communicating to her in detail just how treacherous her behaviour had been, coming as it did on top of Grace's death and the desertion by his 'real' parents, yet despite all his considerable efforts she *still* hadn't come back.

The tapes he'd sent Miriam had been his only vent for the negativity and anger he felt not just towards her, but to life in general. Sometimes he even suffered from amnesia afterwards and couldn't remember exactly what had been on the tape, but he sent them anyway, because she needed to understand the damage she'd done. It was the only honest way forward.

She'd never apologised or attempted to rectify the situation and on the contrary had more than once threatened to cut off contact altogether if he didn't stop, but that defiance had only increased his anger. If she wanted war, then he'd give her a global one.

He wondered if it would be any different if they met up in real life and the idea began to obsess him. *She* wouldn't come back to England so it would be up to him to go out there, but just nipping over to the other side of the world was easier said than done and in a way the idea frightened him because she'd left *14* years ago and they were both different people now. *He* certainly was, at any rate. It was sad, really, to think back to that time when life had held so much promise, yet look at him now.

Since then he'd *passed out* at Sandhurst, had an exemplary six years with the *11th Hussars* in which time he'd travelled the world and risen to the rank of Lieutenant, then embarked on a less successful year in the *Army Air Corps* when he'd nearly killed himself in a helicopter crash, followed by a 1st class degree in Political Science from *The London School of Economics* and now... he was working as a motorcycle courier. Admittedly it wasn't quite where he'd hoped to be by a long shot, although from what he'd picked up over the years, life hadn't been a bunch of roses for Miriam, either.

She'd started off temping, had some or other disastrous love affair with a married man and then done a teaching qualification. If she'd had any relationships since then she hadn't mentioned them and nor had she mentioned any friends. More than anything she talked about the past—the years they'd spent as children in Singapore and Australia during the War and then growing up in Somerset. But while *her* memories were all happy, *rose-tinted-spectacles* stuff, *his* were of being scared, being pushed around from one place to another, bunged in a children's home for a while and then shunted off to two public schools.

In fact, they'd *both* had been packed off to boarding schools and it had worked out rather worse for Miriam than it had for *him*, so she simply wasn't being honest in her recollections and it enraged him. How could she be so disingenuous?! He would *have* to go over there and make her see reason. Accordingly, much of his time had lately been spent mulling over the conundrum of how best to plan such a grand venture. It would, after all, be considerably more complicated than just hopping over to Sheringham.

And then it came to him like a beam of light in the darkness. Of course, he'd do it *properly* and buy a camper van once he was over there—one of those VW things. He might even be able to get there this year if he worked hard and took on overtime, although he'd have to be careful that his visits to Frank weren't affected. Given that they'd both suffered so much at the hands of the same family, it would be an unforgiveable treason for Murray to do the same.

Things were so different with Frank. Murray never felt impatient or angry with him despite—it had to be said—considerable provocation at times. He hadn't yet told him any more about their parents since that first attempt, although Frank hadn't forgotten what he'd said and gloried in the inspired fantasy of his mother being a film star. Murray hadn't tried to disavow him of this enhancement of Grace's talents and also hadn't yet mentioned that she was dead. After all, what did it matter as long as daydreaming about her made Frank happy?

Murray had only been two and a half when Grace had died in the most bizarre freak accident. They'd lived in Australia since February 1942 after escaping the chaos of the Singapore evacuation and at that point had been living in a little wooden house in a small community of ex-pat wives in Frankston—a small, coastal town in Victoria, not far from Melbourne.

It was May 19th, 1943, so they'd been there for around 15 months and their mother, Grace, had already made a name for herself on account of being both beautiful and extrovert. There were lots of parties to keep their spirits up and she played the piano and sang at most of them, but this day was special, because the wives had just heard that their husbands were Japanese prisoners of war in Singapore's *Changi Jail* and weren't dead, as had been feared.

So, they were going out to celebrate and Grace had run a bath, but on testing the water with her right hand before climbing in, she'd received a huge electric shock which burned her arm from hand to elbow, killing her outright.

The first anyone knew of it was when the *Ayah* who they'd brought from Singapore knocked on the door and couldn't get any answer and then eventually she was found, lying dead on the bathroom floor.

His sister Miriam had later told him that the two children weren't told what had happened for some time, but were taken in by an ex-pat friend and neighbour—Lady Christine Saxon-Snell and her two teenage daughters Daphne and Marianne—and had lived with them for the remainder of the War before being shipped back home in August 1945.

Even Claude hadn't known what had happened to Grace for several months, thanks to the machinations of the *War Office*. He'd received notice that a Mrs Woodall had died but didn't know if it was his mother or his wife and neither was there any indication of how it had happened. It wasn't until one of the teenage Saxon-Snell daughters managed to get a message through several months later that he finally learned the victim was Grace, although the circumstances remained a mystery to him until the end of the War.

Miriam didn't seem to mind any of what had happened to them—apart from their mother dying of course—and Murray couldn't understand it. She'd told him that in Singapore the *Ayah* would spend nearly every day with him on the beach and then Miriam would join them after school for a picnic. *Her* memories were all of endless fun, including with the Saxon-Snell family, but where *she* remembered only camaraderie, to Murray it had been uncertainty and angst.

He could see that no one was to blame for their situation—unless one counted Hitler and the Japanese—but it was what came afterwards which was unforgiveable, because on arrival back in England aged nearly 7 and 5 respectively, their father had them sent to some sort of institution for refugee children. Murray couldn't even remember where it was, but they'd both hated it.

He could understand that Claude—having only just arrived back himself after three years of starvation, abuse and deprivation—hadn't been in a fit state to look after them, but he hadn't even *visited.* And where had Aunt Marjorie and Uncle Roland been when they were needed? Murray and Miriam had literally just been dumped.

He could see that there'd be no point in telling Frank any of this because in the first place he'd never be able to understand or take in most of it and in the second place there was no point in potentially distressing him. Curiously he hadn't yet asked about their father, even though Claude *had* occasionally visited him in the past, although probably not for a long time.

Sometimes he thought of just driving down to Somerset and taking everything up with Claude: his true parentage, the goons, the neglect he and Miriam had suffered as children, Frank...

Being both exceptionally bright and athletic, Murray had done very well at public school. He'd gone to *Radley* in Oxfordshire where there was an old well said to be full of the bones of soldiers who'd died in World War I, although he'd never felt inclined to test the theory and nor had anyone else as far as he knew.

However, although his days at one of the most expensive schools in the country hadn't been any great burden, he had a theory that he'd been sent away as a ploy to stop him asking questions about his past and in order to stop him claiming that he'd been singled out, they'd dispatched Miriam as well. And even though poor Miriam wasn't particularly bright and hadn't made friends easily, she *still* didn't resent what they'd done to her.

Claude had found time to get married again in March 1946—almost indecently quickly—and predictably it was to one of the doctors who'd treated him on his return. No doubt it was more convenient for them to be on their own, without a couple of kids from his first marriage knocking around. They'd even had one of their own as well—Julie—and *she'd* never been sent away to school. Funny that.

Soon after moving in with his new wife—Aunt Josephine—Claude had sent for his children to join them, although not Frank. Their first home after the War had been a little thatched cottage in Bishop's Hull, Somerset and with hindsight it had been an idyllic setting, although Murray hadn't appreciated that side of things at the time and especially given that he was away at boarding school most of the time. Moreover, his new stepmother had seemed all right and her salary as a doctor had kept them going after Claude left the Army and took up market gardening.

For many years now Murray had been an adult in his own right, but circumstances still conspired to make him almost more powerless than he had been as a child and meeting up with Frank again had only intensified his sense of injustice and helplessness. He'd established a routine of driving down to Hove twice a week and wished he could go more often, but it was petrol that was the problem—it was just so *expensive*, not to mention that he had to save extra hard if his trip to Australia was ever going to become a reality.

He hadn't yet told anyone about his plans because he wanted it to be a surprise—not an especially nice one, he suspected, and especially not for Miriam who almost certainly thought that the considerable distance and three oceans between them would be enough to deter all but the most determined visitors.

He wondered if the goons would be able to follow him abroad. It was possible that they wouldn't be able to survive altitude, but he hadn't tested it before because they'd only become a problem since his return to England after the helicopter accident. Nor did he know other basic details, such as if they could tolerate immersion in water or even if they needed to breathe.

In a way, life was quite good. He'd been off that ridiculous medication for five months now and Frank could take most of the credit for bringing him back from the edge of the abyss. His job had also helped, because he enjoyed weaving through the streets of London on his motorbike, instinctively knowing the correct routes even when he had to improvise. In fact, that was almost the bit he liked best, solving the puzzle presented by a veritable labyrinth of lanes and alleyways and always coming out on top.

It wasn't intellectually demanding in the traditional sense, but then that wasn't what he wanted just now. After all, it wasn't as if he had anything to prove in that department and when he wasn't with Frank it was time spent on the motorbike which had been instrumental in keeping his negativity and depression at bay.

His irregular timetable also meant that apart from spending time with Frank, he was able to pass long hours visiting art galleries and museums or—when he had a free evening—venturing to the theatre. Against all the odds, he was actually having quite a nice life at the moment, thanks to his own brilliance and ingenuity in overcoming the machinations of others.

But despite periods of respite, Murray knew that he was only counting time and at some point would have to make that trip to Somerset to confront his father. He had some admiration for Claude—emerging alive from *Changi Jail* was no mean feat and he'd even succeeded in re-building his life afterwards, but at what cost to the children from his first marriage and in particular to Murray?

He even wondered sometimes if he might be the illegitimate son of his father's wealthy cousin, *Old Barn*, but somehow couldn't see it. She certainly had brains, but was a very dry old stick and he couldn't imagine *her* having any romantic involvements. Besides, physically she wasn't like Murray at all. No, he had a feeling that his origins were a lot more complicated and lay somewhere further afield than that.

The day came towards the end of January when he found himself faced with either another visit to the *Tate Modern* or an unscheduled visit to Frank and unexpectedly it became the moment of truth—he no longer had an excuse *not* to confront his father with what he knew, because it wasn't only his right, it was his *duty*.

However, he wouldn't be going back into that damned room with the Persian carpet again. Moreover, he'd remain calm this time, whatever happened, but he *had* to bring the truth out into the open.

It was a long journey to Somerset—165 miles and nearly three and a half hours, thanks to the London traffic. However, he was so preoccupied with his objectives that he barely noticed the time and didn't even give a second thought to the countryside changing along the route or the medley of picturesque little villages which he passed through.

Having lived in Bishop's Hull for so long, it had become no more than just another element in the great deception.

The house was the only one in a largely disused country lane, small and pink with a thatch in which all the birds in the area had been partying for decades. The straw was dark with age and so damaged that the surface was uneven all over as if a giant had taken huge and uneven bites out of it, not to mention that there were patches which looked positively wet—and they probably were. Murray couldn't imagine why they didn't get it fixed.

It wasn't the best time of year to see the garden, but he had to admit that it was probably the best thing about the house, which had certainly been too small and cramped when they'd all been living there together in the school holidays. There was a croquet lawn, a tennis court and even a wooded area and as children, he and Miriam had had a field day climbing trees and playing hide & seek.

In addition Claude had also rented a couple of acres nearby where he grew lettuces, tomatoes and cucumbers—possibly more—and sold them at local markets, but Murray had never taken any interest at all in that side of things.

Being back in a place which was so familiar, but to which he no longer belonged was a strange feeling—especially bearing in mind his mission—and he was torn between the pull of what should have been happy memories and the fact that so much of it had been a big lie.

A gravel drive led up to the cottage through a wooded area and he drove along it up to a fork. To go left would take him to the back of the cottage and what would traditionally have been the tradesmen's entrance and to go right would take him to the front of the house, alongside the croquet lawn.

He took the right fork and parked in the driveway, a few yards from the ancient, wooden front door which was shot through with metal studs and looked in a similar state of disarray to the thatch.

He knocked three times and waited, listening to sounds of life from within and then his stepmother Josephine opened the door. For a few moments she stared at him, her face drained of colour and he felt immediately irritated. 'Nice to see you, too, Aunt Josephine,' he said, trying not to over-do the sarcasm at such an early stage, because that wouldn't have been conducive to the visit being a success.

She recovered enough to make a vague gesture of kissing his cheek, but to his relief stopped well short of touching him. 'Murray, I'm so sorry. It's just such a shock. Why didn't you tell us you were coming? I'd have got in something for lunch if I'd known.'

No more keeping up appearances. Be honest. 'It's all right, Aunt, I only came to speak to my father, not for lunch.'

A modicum of alarm flickered across her expression, but she quickly ushered him inside and covered any confusion with banalities. 'Come through, darling and sit in the drawing room while I get you a drink.'

He flinched at the endearment, although she'd always called he and Miriam 'darling' as she also did to other family members and even friends. He'd almost forgotten that.

The cottage inside was bigger than it looked from the outside and was beamed throughout in both the walls and ceilings—it was said with wood salvaged from an 18th century shipwreck—and Murray sat down on an old, two-seater sofa which came roughly in the same category of hazardous upholstery as Aunt Marjorie's billowing old thing.

Fortunately, this room wasn't home to the offending Persian carpet which had played such an unexpected and obtrusive role in his previous visit—that was next door in Claude's study. All the same, Murray didn't feel very comfortable. It was cold and the adjacent open fire was unlit, although ready prepped with dry logs and rolled up newspapers.

Josephine seemed to be following his thought processes as she said suddenly, 'I'll get some matches and you can get the fire going, then I'll make us a drink.'

She hurried out of the room and Murray heard her talking in a low murmur—

on the phone, he thought, judging by the faint 'ting' at the end as she replaced the receiver—and then in a short time she was back with the matches.

'I've rung your father. He's over at the market garden, but he'll come back and see you...' she faltered, thrust the matches into his hands and disappeared again, presumably to make the promised cup of tea.

Murray knelt down by the fireplace and lit a roll of newspaper before teasing the flames into life with a pair of battered old bellows. He'd made quite good headway by the time Josephine came back with a tray on which was a teapot, along with three of those familiar mint-green cups and saucers of the type that were everywhere, these days. They'd always used mugs in the past, but he didn't mention it.

When sugar and milk had been allocated to the satisfaction of both parties and they'd taken their initial, genteel sips, Josephine said, 'I realise you want to talk to Claude on his own, but I beg you to keep calm. He's not strong either mentally or physically and after you left the last time he was very upset. He's been through an awful lot, as you know.'

He looked at her critically. 'So have *I* been through an awful lot.'

She said nothing, but he read a great deal in her expression and knew that she was fearful of antagonising him. However, far from having the desired, calming effect, it only made him even more resolute.

Carefully she replaced the cup in its saucer. 'That was all I wanted to say. So, whatever it is... just please stay calm. I've said exactly the same to your father.'

At that moment the rattle of Claude's *Landrover* was heard in the drive and they waited in silence as he made his way through the front door and into the room, dwarfing it with his 6 foot 4 inches and stooping slightly to avoid hitting his head on the beams. Inexplicably it irritated Murray that he himself wasn't sufficiently tall to have encountered that particular problem.

'I've made tea for you darling, but you can pour it yourself.'

He nodded in a gesture which spoke volumes and she hurried out, closing the door behind her.

Claude sat down and nodded to Murray. 'Hello. You've certainly caught us on the hop today. I don't normally come back for lunch these days.'

He spoke quietly, but then he was a very quiet man—shy even—and quite the opposite of his extrovert first wife. Given Grace's beauty and charisma it was understandable that he'd fallen in love with her, but Miriam had said that she remembered them having explosive rows when they'd been out in Singapore. It was hard to imagine now, with Claude being so quiet.

His hair was grey now, but at least he still had plenty of it and was a good-looking man in many respects with fine bone structure, intense blue-grey eyes and a firm chin. The market gardening business must be keeping him in good shape as well, because although his shoulders were slightly bowed—possibly a reflection of his great height—he hadn't noticeably put on any weight at all. Murray looked at him critically. Physically or otherwise, the two of them were so completely unalike that it beggared belief to imagine they could be related.

Many years ago, Jospehine had told himself and Miriam that when Claude first returned to England in 1945 he was yellow from the malaria pills issued by the British Army, not to mention skeletal from three years of eating nothing more than tiny amounts of rice. Derisory amounts of other food had been available, but he'd rejected them on the basis that they were likely to be infected with something or other and had been vindicated by the deaths of countless starving comrades who'd taken that risk at their peril.

His work clothes now comprised faded dungarees and a home-made, blue, woolly jumper. His Wellingtons were presumably by the front door as his size 11 feet were clothed only in green, patterned socks.

Murray took a deep breath. The crackling fire and peace in the room made his job more difficult because discord was always jarring, but having come all this way he couldn't hold back. 'I'm sorry our last meeting ended so badly. It wasn't what I intended.'

Claude was noticeably tense, but after a pause he said, 'You can ask me anything you want, but although I'll answer you truthfully, it won't necessarily be what you want to hear.'

A shadow passed across Murray's face. It was as if he'd been fobbed off even before the first questions had passed his lips and he tried to control the anger which was bubbling away inside him. 'First, I beg you to tell me the secret of my true parentage. I've always known that my real family is not this one, despite the great lengths you went to in trying to keep it from me. The hypnosis, sending me away to school... I'm willing to admit that in most cases your precautions would probably have been sufficient, but my exceptional intellect alerted me to what was happening at a very early age.'

He stopped and waited for Claude to speak.

'Is that it?'

Murray managed to control himself. 'No, but I think it's enough to start with.'

Claude visibly braced himself. 'All right. I *am* your real father and believe me when I tell you that I really wish I could tell you otherwise. However, unfortunately for both of us, it's the truth and if you took the medication for your schizophrenia, you wouldn't have the psychosis which puts all these false ideas about hypnosis and God knows what else into your head. There may have been a time when you managed without treatment, but the helicopter accident made things a lot worse and now you really need to deal with it. I know I've said all this before, but there's nothing else I can say.'

Murray heard himself shouting as if from a distance. 'But the goons you send to spy on me are real enough. You're just trying to make me lose my mind so that I believe all your shit. What's the real motive, hey? Is there an inheritance I've been cheated out of, is that it?!'

He could feel himself shaking all over and forced himself to stop, but the demons had been unleashed and he was almost terrified himself as to where it would all end.

Claude leaned forwards and spoke quietly, his voice uncompromising. 'The goons—as you call them—are part of your condition. It's called psychosis and they don't exist except in your imagination. Take your medication and they'll disappear. What reason could I *possibly* have for spying on you? And what makes you think that I have any sort of access to the magic necessary to conjure up such creatures?

This was going the same way as their last conversation and it seemed to Murray that there was a dark cavern opening up before him, from which there was no escape. Life loomed before him as a void and he felt helpless, even worthless, a nobody without the reinforcement of a family name that he could call his own.

He was on the point of launching himself across the coffee table and physically attacking Claude, when Josephine entered and broke the crackle of negative energy which was seesawing between them with frightening velocity.

'I'm sorry I can't help you, Murray. You can only help yourself by starting your medication again,' said Claude.

Murray scrambled to his feet as best he could in defiance of the efforts of the sofa to detain him and screamed, 'But it's a lie, all a lie!' He was sufficiently in possession of his faculties to be a little fearful of what he might do and it flashed through his head that he could have killed both of them with little chance of ever being apprehended. However, some primeval inhibition prevented him from enacting that fantasy and in frustration he snatched up a teacup and hurled it across the room at a portrait of Elizabeth I before rushing outside and screeching to a halt in the driveway, breathing heavily.

Helplessly he batted at the empty air, cursing the goons which were weaving around him like triumphant genies released from a bottle, until with a cry of anguish he hurled himself into the driving seat of the *Herald* and careered down the drive so erratically that he only missed colliding with a tree by a fraction of an inch and hurtled onto the public highway in similarly precarious fashion. Only at that point did Fate relent and give him a good mile and a half of empty country lane in which to gather together his scrambled wits before the challenges of the main road presented themselves.

Back in the cottage, Claude wiped a tear from his cheek. 'I'll probably have to answer for this at *St Peter's Gate*, but I wish he'd never been born. Why can't the mad bastard just take his bloody medication and leave us in peace?'

His wife sighed. 'He's obsessed with coming from wealthy and titled origins and can't let go of that aspiration. It's not good enough for him to be plain Murray Woodall and if he takes the medication then he loses the fantasy that he craves, so we're in a *Catch 22* situation.'

Claude took her hand. 'I just wonder if we could have done anything at all—something different along the way—which would have...'

Josephine cut him off. 'Claude, please don't torture yourself. We know that there was mental instability in Grace's family and that sort of thing gets passed down the generations. It's happened again with his cousin—Poor Marjorie's been at her wits' end over Tristan's depression, yet both boys have had every possibly advantage when they were growing up. If Murray refuses to believe that he's schizophrenic and won't take his medication then it's very sad, but there's absolutely nothing you could have done to prevent it.'

She bent down and started to pick up pieces of smashed teacup from the carpet, noting with relief that it had smashed against the wall, rather than the portrait. It was rather ironic that Murray had chosen to vent his frustration on the *Virgin Queen* as that was one woman who could have eaten him for breakfast and at the very least would have had his head on a plate.

Claude put his head in his hands. It was such a waste—that forensic intelligence, the fine Army career in a cavalry regiment, a first-class degree from a top university. Polo, fast cars, theatres, travelling the world. He'd had it all and yet it had come to this. It was such a damned shame. And worst of all was that to his own great mortification, Murray's own father wished him dead—not in a bad way, but like a mercy killing. Anything, anything at all which would put both of them out of their misery.

Chapter 5

Christmas Eve 1974
Darwin, Australia
Murray closed the portacabin door rather reluctantly, as he now had before him one and a half days to fill while the *Casnarma* building site was closed. He would have elected to work on *Christmas Day* as well if he could, but at least the compulsory closures only amounted to that single day, so things could have been worse.

So far, he'd been very lucky. In the end he'd left England in September and flown first to India, travelling initially to Delhi and then down the central state of Rajasthan, calling in at some of the country's most famous landmarks: the famous and ancient city of Jaipur which was fashioned in beautiful, rose-coloured stone, the resplendent *Taj Majal* in Agra, the astonishing *Lake Palace Hotel* in Udaipur and then that most impressive relic of the British in India—Chittorgarh, where an enormous fort dwarfed the surrounding countryside.

He'd even stayed a couple of nights in the splendidly dilapidated, post-colonial town of Bundi, where dusty chandeliers hung by a thread and the waiters still bowed. It was now a very neglected outpost and anyone calling there was usually using it merely as a stopover to bridge the six-hour journey between Jaipur to the north and Chittorgarh to the south, but in fact he'd really enjoyed it there. Certainly, the dignified echoes of all that pomp and splendour had been far preferable to another of his stopovers, namely Ahmedabad, where the children threw stones with disconcerting accuracy at any foreign bodies. Murray's indignant response to these assaults on his person had been to privately label the place as *Ahmedabad-to-worse*, although to his great disappointment it was a joke which he was unable to share with any other visitors for the simple reason that there *weren't* any.

However, best of all had been Bombay, where he'd stayed a whole six weeks because he loved it so much and he'd even treated himself to a week in the *Taj Majal Palace Hotel*. Everything was so cheap that he'd lived like a king throughout his time in India, although even that hadn't been enough to keep him completely well all the time. He'd been very careful: drinking only bottled water and avoiding fresh fruit and vegetables, but personally he attributed his good health to an old and very well-travelled lady he'd met in Delhi, who had advised him to swig down a medicinal glass of brandy every night. She'd insisted that it would kill most evil bacteria stone dead and with a couple of brief, but unpleasant exceptions this enjoyable preventative seemed to have been very effective..

He'd taken a flight from Bombay to Darwin because travelling from Bombay it was a shorter flight to northern Australia, so it made sense to start there and travel south west down the country towards Sydney, taking in as many other hotspots as possible along the way—Alice Springs, Ayer's Rock, Perth, Cairns, the Gold Coast, Melbourn, Frankston and Sydney—not necessarily in that order. Unfortunately, those places were by no means in a convenient straight line and Perth in furthermost Western Australia was a staggering 2,500 miles out of his way including the return route, but all the same he'd set his heart on experiencing its vast stretches of unspoiled, sandy beaches.

The one thing he *was* certain of was that Sydney would be his last port of call before returning home after thousands of miles of driving and possibly a couple of inland flights as well. That was where he and Miriam would meet for the first time in 15 years, but he'd cross that bridge when he came to it and for now had pushed the prospect to the back of his mind with an apprehension which surprised him.

'Face your demons, face your demons...' was a mantra he repeated sternly to himself whenever he remembered, but luckily there was usually something more immediate demanding his attention and so far he'd managed to avoid reverting to the black moods which had plagued him in England. Moreover, he was having such a good time on this trip that he really didn't want to think about Miriam, for fear of where it would lead.

Right now, Murray was resigned to passing the time as best he could until work started again, but with *Cyclone Tracey* moving towards Darwin, they might be in for a lively time of it over Christmas, so perhaps his camper van would be the best place to be after all. Thank God he'd thought to buy some books in India—at least he'd have plenty to read.

It was just after midday and it had begun to rain steadily, but the shops were still open and Murray needed to buy food, so he started walking in the direction of a small row of shops, one of which was a supermarket he'd used before.

It was amazing how everything had fallen into place since his arrival at the beginning of December. His initial objective had been to search for a camper van and in the first newspaper he'd looked at, there had been one in the small ads—60,000 miles on the clock and price $1400, which worked out at around £825.

It was orange with a white roof and his first thought was how much Frank would have loved it, even though it wasn't quite yellow. Even better, it was being sold by a garage in central Darwin and came with guarantees, although as he'd probably be thousands of miles away by the time anything went wrong, he didn't set too much store by that. It was a fearful amount of money to spend, but it was love at first sight and he was also hopeful of getting most of that money back when he sold it again at the end of his journey. He'd been in Darwin less than three hours before it became his, so didn't even have to spend a single night in a hotel.

His run of luck had continued with the discovery of a suitable caravan camp in the northern suburbs where he could park for the equivalent of £2 a week and then within three days he'd found work on the *Casnarma* building site where he planned to earn as much as possible over the course of a few weeks in order to fund the rest of his trip.

His first port of call would probably be the central, desert destination of Alice Springs—just to say he'd been, really—and that alone was a drive of over 900 miles. He'd have to take his time.

There'd been quite a lot of talk about cyclones over the last 48 hours or so, but no one was worried as they seldom came close to land and usually resulted in nothing more than a couple of days of heavy rain. One such had occurred three weeks previously and the town had been hit with a torrential 12 inches of rain over 72 hours, but the last cyclone to actually hit Darwin had occurred 20 years previously and even then not much damage was done.

Murray reached the little supermarket and wandered along the aisles, wondering what to buy for Christmas lunch. Cooking facilities on the camper van were necessarily limited, so in the end he bought a cooked chicken that would hopefully last for a few meals and also some potatoes and carrots. The veggies would have to be boiled rather than roasted, but that couldn't be helped.

He also topped up on cereal which was always good for a snack, plus milk and chocolate. It all came to less than $3, so he felt he'd done rather well.

It was a 15-minute walk to the camp but the bag wasn't heavy and at the moment the rain wasn't too bad either, although it looked like being a fairly dull 24 hours or so in every sense of the word.

Murray was quite surprised when he turned on the radio an hour or so later to find that the presenters were full of precautions regarding an anticipated cyclone, but then realised that this was standard procedure and didn't actually mean anything was going to happen. He wondered whether to take down the camper van's pop-up roof just as a precaution. This normally served as his bedroom, but he decided to go ahead anyway, just in case, and sleep on one of the bunks instead.

The radio warnings were forecasting winds of 120 mph gusting to 150 mph, this being considered severe but not catastrophic. All the same, Murray began to feel a little uncomfortable and peered out of the window to see if there was any movement in the camp. However, no one else seemed worried and there were still plenty of vehicles around. It was now getting rather late to leave in any case, although the cyclone's distance and rate of movement had it crossing the coastline at 6 am on Christmas morning—the next day—so anyone prepared to travel overnight would still have plenty of time to escape the worse of it.

He made himself a cup of tea with water boiled in the pan and a dash of the milk that he'd just bought and mulled over the comforting notion that this lifestyle was really quite civilised, so long as one kept one's tastes simple.

It occurred to him that he was parked quite near to a short, stocky tree which was one of several around the outskirts of the camp site and that this might prove to be a hazard if the wind got as bad as was predicted. However, if he went forwards he'd be encroaching on to someone else's pitch and to go backwards would have put him near a veritable *row* of trees, so he decided to leave well alone. Anyway, what with all the hype about the imminent cyclone, he'd asked the owner's wife about the trees a few days ago and she'd reassured him that all the rotten ones had been cut down months ago, so there was no threat. He was pacified.

Besides, it was getting dark and the rain was heavier now—two very good reasons for doing nothing.

He'd been hoping to go to sleep at about 9 pm as usual and sleep through it all, but as the wind's howling grew in volume and was accompanied by a deluge of rain, he lost his nerve and instead sat trying to read a book on Hindu art, which he'd bought in Bombay.

The radio cut out at about 9.30 pm—he supposed that meant the mast was down—and he resigned himself to a long night, but then the status quo was shattered at about midnight when with the wind at a good gale force, there was a resounding crash and the van shook violently.

Murray realised instantly that the tree must have struck the van after all, but given that the VW was still apparently in one piece he didn't dare get out to look and could only hope that it was the higher, less solid portion of the tree which was responsible. Either way, it appeared to have struck towards the front and with a bit of luck his little black, metal trunk in the luggage space would have saved the roof from the worst of it.

It seemed very odd for a tree to fall onto one's vehicle and not to be able to do anything about it, but he knew that as long as the van stayed intact, it was the safest place to be. In fact, the tree might even have done him a favour as its branches would hopefully now be acting as a buffer against the wind and indeed against anything else falling in his direction.

Peering out through the branches of the tree canopy which now enveloped the VW, he could see that there was dense rain travelling horizontally over the ground and the van shook along with the tree to the accompaniment of an occasional muffled crash from other parts of the camp site.

His heart thumping, Murray sat tight and listened. It felt a bit like a game of *Dare*, sitting and waiting for his turn to come around again, although the protection afforded by the branches of the tree went some way towards reassuring him.

It was a long night and the buffeting didn't let up, then at about 4 am when the wind lessened slightly, he slid open the door of the van and on emerging through the branches was amazed to see via flashes of sheet lightning that one caravan was smashed upside down on top of its neighbour, while another had been bowled over several yards onto the dirt track which ran through the park. Meanwhile, the surrounding trees which were still standing had without exception been either denuded of their branches altogether or completely stripped of foliage.

Seeing it all in this way via lightning was quite unearthly and Murray wondered if this was what *Armageddon* would be like and how they'd feel back home if his number was up, this very night. Relieved, probably. Guilty or sorry? Almost certainly not.

A fresh wave of driving rain prevented him from becoming any more maudlin just at that moment and he rushed back into the van, scratching his face on the tree branches as he sprinted through and slammed the door shut.

Murray leaned back on his bunk—which was designed more for lying than for sitting—and tried to induce a half-sleep which would make the time pass more quickly, but by the time dawn broke at around 7 am he felt pale and drawn and imagined he looked it, too. Initially he couldn't see anything due to the semi-darkness and the branches blocking his view, but at 8 am decided to risk venturing out for a quick reconnaissance.

He slid open the doors to a bare minimum in order to squeeze out and after edging through the foliage was rewarded with evidence that his little trunk *had* taken most of the force of the tree trunk and without that stroke of luck the roof of the camper van would almost certainly have caved in. From what he could see, the roof at that point was a little dented and the fibreglass moulded top was cracked, but otherwise everything seemed OK and given that the rain was still torrential he felt particularly fortunate that against all the odds the VW's windows were still intact.

He saw that his neighbour had also braved the wind and rain to make a similar inspection, but the outcome for him wasn't so encouraging as *his* caravan had actually been shunted up at about 20 degrees by the upturned roots of the same tree which had hit Murray's camper van. It went through his mind to try and get to a phone box and call for help, but what possible help was going to come out in this? And besides, the lines would almost certainly be down.

At that point the wind was still one continuous roar with occasional surges and suddenly losing his nerve again, he hurried back inside the open door of the van, holding on to the branches as he went, lest the wind whip him away like *Mary Poppins.*

By around midday the wind had dropped a little as Darwin entered the eye of the cyclone and feeling rather like a mole coming up for air, Murray cautiously ventured forth once more. A pre-fab cabin which had looked fairly solid earlier that morning, now appeared to have moved several feet closer to his van and after staring at it mesmerised for a full minute, he impulsively accepted the offer of a lift from some chaps in the neighbouring caravan who were moving out in two cars.

He leapt into the back of the first car, only to almost immediately regret it as the vehicle cut a ridiculously jagged path out of the camp, its path impeded by a forest of fallen branches and debris, followed by floodwater which completely did for the car behind, causing its brakes to fail so that it drove straight into the back of the first.

The off-side wing of the second car was completely buckled and the driver was forced to abandon ship—almost literally given the deluge of water all around them—and clutching a sizeable Alsatian puppy he half-fell, half was bundled into the back seat of the first car, sandwiching Murray in between the newcomer and another man.

The newcomer—who said his name was Dave—had a deep cut in his arm but seemed remarkably cheerful, all things considered. He'd been at a party in a nearby house until the building had been split in two by the storm, at which point the merrymakers had scattered. Murray decided that the man might have been less chilled were it not for the booze still permeating his veins. The puppy fortunately behaved impeccably and smelled a lot better than Dave did.

It was a slow and tedious business negotiating the flood water, even though the distance to the centre couldn't have been more than a couple of miles. However, probably at about the half-way juncture and just as they were entering the edge of the town, the relatively light breeze metamorphosed into a fat, roaring storm in the space of a few seconds, the rain blotting out the view like fog and necessarily bringing the car to a standstill.

The windscreen quietly collapsed and the rear windscreen followed suit as Murray and the other four occupants—plus dog—did their best to huddle down behind the dashboard and front seats as gravel and detritus flew around them, carried along with the rain. Worryingly, there was also a good deal of corrugated iron flying about and they could only pray that none of it would hit their car.

They stayed hunkered down for two hours, waiting for the wind to lessen before deciding to abort the mission and move back to camp, offloading Dave and dog to an undamaged car that they met along the way. The destruction now clearly on view was amazing—steel girders bent to the ground, many houses completely demolished and none having escaped entirely.

Houses in that part of the world were principally built on stilts made of concrete and constructed with asbestos and plaster within a wooden frame topped by corrugated iron roofs, so they weren't particularly strong and *Cyclone Tracey* had cut a swathe through most of them, leaving only the concrete pillars standing. Wreckage was everywhere and even brick walls had been blown down.

On arrival back at the park, the damage was even worse than when they'd left, with some caravans having disappeared altogether and the rest smashed. The pre-fab which had occasioned Murray some concern earlier after moving a few feet towards his VW, was now about 50 yards away in the middle of a pile of smashed caravans.

Amazingly, the camper van was worse off by only a few scratches and a broken window, the fallen tree and overhanging branches having done a sterling job of protecting it—including from the broken caravan next door, parts of which were now skewered in its branches, whereas they would otherwise have smashed straight into the van.

Murray made some coffee for his ex-neighbours who now had nowhere to go and as the afternoon wore on, residents began returning, most of them having left at some point during the day.

The consensus was generally amazement and relief that they were still alive and largely unhurt, although many were already worrying about insurance—or lack of it—and how they were going to manage in the meantime.

By now many people were out sightseeing—including from outside the camp—and survival stories were already being exchanged, so with nothing else to do, Murray stood listening to them for a while until driven by hunger he returned to the VW and tucked into his Christmas lunch of cooked roast chicken and accompaniments. As power cables and other infrastructure were out of action, most people in the town were completely without any means of cooking, so for once those on the campsite were better off as most used *Calor Gas*. However, whether they were able to access it amid the wreckage of their caravans was another matter.

The radio was off air until *Boxing Day* afternoon which was a nuisance, but when it finally did return, it became a round-the-clock focus of information and instruction. Apparently, the town's wind speed indicators had broken at 190 knots—about 250 mph—and *Cyclone Tracey* was now in the history books as the third most powerful cyclone recorded, the other two having been in South America.

Another story going about was that Police had found the clear imprint of a refrigerator 50 foot up on the side of a water tower, although Murray had reservations about that. How on earth could they possibly know that it had been a refrigerator unless it had helpfully imprinted its logo and serial number?

Rather more reliable was the information that debris had been spotted by aircraft up to 40 miles away.

Amazingly only 70 people had died, although hundreds had been injured and the consensus was that these figures would have been much worse had the full force of the cyclone not hit until after dark, for which reason most people had sat tight—as Murray had—so keeping casualties down.

Murray left it three days before returning to the *Casnarma* building site in central Darwin, only to find that the workshop, huts and offices had either disappeared or were smashed up and there was a good ten feet of water in the excavated area. Nor were any foremen present at the main office, so glumly he turned around and walked back home again. After the heady 24-hour excitement between Christmas Eve and Christmas Day, life post-*Cyclone Tracey* had become extremely boring.

However, he was able to put that afternoon to good use by finally getting the tree lifted off the van with the help of a local government crane which had been dispatched to the site and was encouraged to discover that the van worked just as well as it had done before all the drama. Even the lift-up section of the roof was operating all right, so he had his sleeping quarters back. The severely dented black trunk had also done a sterling job in protecting most of its contents—including all Murray's precious photographs of India.

The next day he moved to a more central site at *Darwin High School*, this having become one of the main flood and evacuation centres. He had to admit that once it got going, state support was first class—meals were free, all sorts of canned foods were given out free and the mass catering was so good that Murray was eating far better than he had done before. There were also film shows every night in the aftermath and even a couple of concerts given by a folk group called the *Seekers* who flew in from Victoria to raise morale.

Having already begun to feel moderately cheerful, Murray's cup became full to overflowing with work on the building site picking up much sooner than expected. On returning only the day after his initial visit he was gratified to find it a hive of activity and was accordingly checked into one of several teams who were being dispatched on re-roofing jobs around the town.

In his own case a team of four went to the *Leper Hospital* and work there lasted a couple of days before continuing onto a bakery, then a hotel and then several normal houses, of which there were a seemingly unlimited supply.

By the time a couple of weeks had passed the worst was over, but the cost of rebuilding was estimated at a painful $150-200 million, with a timescale of several years. However, in the meantime the government rashly or generously—whichever way you looked at it—committed to covering the cost of repairs where there was no insurance, meaning that even Murray's minor repairs to the VW would be covered.

Moreover, his assistance in helping to patch up buildings entitled him to two weeks paid holiday and two free flights anywhere in Australia. It simply couldn't have worked out better if he'd planned it and one way or another, he was a lot better off after *Cyclone Tracey* than he had been before. In the few weeks that he'd been in Australia he'd already managed to save over $1,000.

However, he instinctively resisted giving any outward indication of just how convenient this crisis was for him, being well aware that he was fortunate to have got off very lightly. For most people the event had been far more expensive, not to mention all the accounts of harrowing experiences and severe injuries. In fact, such was the elation of simply still being alive that Murray even thawed sufficiently towards his distant family to send Aunt Marjorie a letter which not only conveyed his survival but also honoured her with a blow-by-blow account of everything that had happened. He conferred on her the responsibility of informing the rest of the family and even provided a P.O. box address that any of them could reply to while he was still in Darwin.

His familial duties completed, he still worried about Frank. If he wrote him a letter, perhaps one of the staff would read it to him, but he was reluctant to involve anyone else in their relationship or do anything which might risk the family getting to hear about it.

Thankfully the goons didn't seem to have followed him abroad—either in India or Australia—and he'd felt remarkably clear-headed for the entire duration of the trip, which only confirmed that when left to himself he managed just fine. All that baloney about medication...well, it just proved how wrong his father was and when things went tits-up it was invariably the result of outside forces working against him in league with senior family members.

This trip was a welcome respite from all that, but he nevertheless kept an eye out for enemy movement, because experience had taught him that it paid to be vigilant.

Chapter 6

August 1975
Tweedale Street, Sydney, Australia
Miriam sat at the desk in her little study, staring at two sets of letters in front of her, one from Murray which was in the small pile comprising only two communications and another more voluminous pile from Aunt Marjorie and Josephine.

She felt very nervous. These reports about Murray weren't good and she was well aware that he'd changed far more even than she had herself, which was quite something—and not for the better, by all accounts. Receiving those tapes from him had been bad enough, but they'd be like a walk in the park compared to having the real thing breathing fire on her doorstep.

When she'd left England in 1960 it really had just been because she wanted to travel and at that stage she hadn't intended to stay away for ever, because she had many, many happy childhood memories of England. However, on moving to Australia she'd almost immediately discovered an unexpected and delicious sense of freedom which had never left her even after 15 years and it was clear to her very early on that barring some sort of disaster, she'd never be going back. Previously it had never had anything to do with Murray, but what with the tapes that she'd been receiving and ominous family accounts, he alone was now a very good reason to stay as far away from England as possible.

Money had been a bit of a problem for a while in the first few years out here—mainly because she'd never had enough of it—but even that had receded after she'd started teaching business in a local secondary school and philosophy in adult evening classes. Effectively she now had the money, the house and her cat, Calypso, who was a beautiful tabby and white male cat with *Omar Sharif* eyes and a disposition which far outclassed that of any man she'd ever met.

And completing the household was 3-legged greyhound Bella who was black with a white bib and although timid and self-effacing to a fault, had made herself quite indispensable over the two years of their acquaintance. Miriam had rescued her from a very basic refuge out in the sticks and the traumatised dog had proved to be quite the best therapy in what was essentially a lonely life. She walked well on three legs, having lost most of the remaining limb in a trap somewhere in the *Blue Mountains* outside Sydney when just a few months old, but beyond that her story would never be known. It was enough that they'd found each other and after an initial huff lasting several days, even Calypso had backed down and accepted her into the household.

She'd originally gone out to Australia with her friend Phyllis, who'd been promised some sort of physiotherapy placement at *Sydney Hospital* and Miriam had simply tagged along with the intention of doing temping. It had been wonderful fun, sharing a flat together, delighting in the temperate climate, new friends, sunbathing on *Bondi Beach*... But then Phyllis had decided to go back when her two-year secondment was up and Miriam had decided to stay.

It wouldn't be an exaggeration to say that the decision to stay had rather brought her down to earth, because she'd missed Phyllis terribly and in an effort to become financially solvent had been forced to drop temping, although that hadn't been any hardship as she'd become fed up of it by then in any case. Instead, she'd signed up for a teacher training course with a bit of help from Daddy—who'd basically paid for it—and hadn't looked back since.

The course had been difficult at times because she wasn't bright like Murray and throughout their schooldays that unequal distribution of brainpower had struck her as horribly unfair. However, having since seen the awful flip side of his forensic intelligence, she'd come to gladly accept her rather average IQ and considered herself extremely fortunate to have escaped a similar fate. Anyway, one way or another she'd got through the course and had been very fortunate since then.

Despite training as an English teacher she'd somehow ended up teaching business studies, a development which meant that her pupils were sixth formers who were generally well- behaved and eager to learn. Initially she hadn't given this much thought, but subsequent horror stories from colleagues who taught lower down the school had brought home to her that without any effort on her own part, she'd been extraordinarily lucky. And that luck had brought in just about enough money to enable her to live on her own in Sydney—a city she'd loved from the start—before finally getting a mortgage three years ago on this little house in the eastern suburbs.

Contrary to initial indications, in the end it wasn't money which had nearly brought her down but disastrous love affairs—two of them, as if she hadn't learned her lesson the first time. Lightening had struck twice in the sense that both had been with married men and were so demoralising that she'd since sworn to be done with romance, lock stock and barrel. It was all over now—one had lasted four years and the other just eight months, with a respite of 18 months between them.

He'd ended the first one after his wife found out and Miriam had ended the second one because it was heading the same way and she couldn't bear the thought of going through it all again. She'd certainly learned her lesson now and it had left her a sadder and wiser person, but she rationalised that it was absolutely for the best, because being young and carefree exposed one to so much pain and disappointment. Far better to be older, careworn and inured to romantic love—there was so much else to life, after all.

That second affair, curiously, had ended on the same day as Murray's helicopter crash in January 1970 and she sometimes wondered if there'd been something in the stars that day.

It wasn't until she'd got this house three years ago and waved goodbye to rental accommodation that she'd been at liberty to look for a cat and had returned from the municipal animal shelter with Calypso. From that moment they'd lived in harmony and it wouldn't be an understatement to say that he'd healed her, so that she was genuinely content to have cast her lot in with the *singletons* of this world. And Bella's arrival had only confirmed what she and Calypso already knew—that one human per household was quite enough.

Since graduating to the status of home-owner she'd thrown herself into teaching and what free time she had was generally spent at home. If she'd learned one thing it was that it didn't do to dwell on the past and that was one reason why those tapes from Murray had been so ghastly, because having just about got her own life together, the last thing she wanted was him blaming her for anything and everything that had gone wrong in *his* life.

Those tapes had become particularly bad after he'd finished his degree and it reached a point where she could hardly bear to play them. They were so alternately angry, despairing and black, black, black all the way through that they threatened to drag her down into the same hopeless pit as him, which was really unfair when she'd done so much to get her life on the level.

And besides that, he talked such a lot of absolute, bloody drivel that quite often she wasn't sure what he was talking about. It was a lot of very big words in sentences which sounded as if they should make grammatical sense, and yet at the end of it she didn't actually know what he was trying to say. It was a bit like when she'd visited France and other people were talking among themselves—having studied the language at school she'd recognised most of the individual words and yet despite this had rarely caught the meaning of an entire sentence.

However, it had been clear that a lot of the time Murray was talking about being done out of something or other—usually money. In the last one he'd made a big thing about it being *his* conceptual and mathematical idea that had produced the first electronic computer, *Colossus* in 1942, but did he not realise that he was only two years old at that time? Certainly, he'd have loved to be acclaimed a biological miracle in some capacity, but if that day ever came it was highly unlikely to have anything to do with *Colossus*.

There were other outrageous claims that he was making to do with copyrights regarding art and music which lost her completely and when he got onto politics—well, she hadn't got a clue about that, either.

Everyone in the family felt so helpless about it because there was nothing one could do to make a grown man—and especially a stubborn one like Murray—take his medication if he didn't want to.

The prospect of being alone with him in the house frightened her. What might he do if he got angry—which he inevitably would do as he got angry with everybody in the family to varying degrees and usually fairly quickly. He also hadn't told her how long he was planning to stay and although she'd reluctantly made up a bed for him, it was a comfort to know that if the worst came to the worst the camper van would be close by and he could go there instead.

Aunt Marjorie hadn't held back in her letter of a year ago, which had been Murray's last social visit to anyone in the family, not counting that awful scene with Daddy and Josephine a few months later when he'd narrowly missed smashing a teacup against that oil painting of Elizabeth I. People had been beheaded for less.

Dated January 1974, Marjorie had written of their Christmas celebration:

...I have to confess that the only blot on it all was Murray. We'd invited him for December 23rd and I think he'd probably still be here, had we not made it very clear that he was expected to leave on 27th.

We all make every possible allowance for him as you know, but now he's really become very difficult and utterly selfish, self-centred, ungrateful and downright lazy. I hate to say it, but it's the truth. He's got quite a good job and plenty of money, but despite all that he seems to have become very 'left' and is an awful sponger. A lot of the time he just stood about doing nothing while we were all running around either cooking or clearing up and we had quite a bust up about it one evening—one of several of varying degrees, I'm afraid, and I wasn't the only one.

His poor, darling mother, how grieved she would be. I'm just so relieved that marvellous old Aunt Barn (isn't she 90 now?) is supposed to be leaving you both a lot of money, so I hope he might be appeased by that, although I doubt it will change his character. It's all so sad and I do feel that the helicopter crash has a lot to do with what's going on, yet his brain must be all right or he couldn't have got his degree? I wish I could understand it...

The letters weren't all about Murray, but they did tend to focus on him rather a lot—quite as much when he *hadn't* been in touch with the family for ages as when he had—but Miriam didn't mind. Too much news was better than no news at all and she also understood that Marjorie didn't really have anyone sufficiently close to Murray that she could talk to about him. Inevitably Roland, Triss and Evie would be getting their share of it as well, but no one had known him as well as Miriam, who had been both mother and big sister to him in those early, crazy days in Singapore and Australia.

Murray couldn't remember Singapore at all—having been only two when they'd left—and Miriam had only hazy memories of it, but the *Ayah* that they'd taken with them to Australia had kept them entertained with lots of stories. They'd lost touch with her after coming back to England and she would have loved to try and trace her, but without even a surname to go on it was an impossible task.

She felt suddenly weary and would have liked to go out for a walk, but with no idea what time Murray would be arriving, she was pretty much stuck here. It would be just her luck that if she even popped out for half an hour, that would be when he arrived and then there'd be hell to pay when she got back and he'd been kept waiting.

Calypso seemed to know that something was bothering her and sat patiently by her feet, rubbing his cheek against her leg in a flattering gesture of possession. She'd read in a book once that when cats did that it was marking the object as their own and she couldn't have been happier that he regarded her as a possession.

She'd made a decision in advance not to contradict Murray if he started talking about being someone other than Murray Woodall—because of course he was bound to talk about it at some point—although some aspects of this confused her, because his conviction obviously meant that he didn't regard her as his real sister, although he'd never yet mentioned anything so specific.

She decided to steel herself and listen to the last tape again, sent in August 1974 shortly before he'd left Britain. In fact, it hadn't been nearly as bad as some of the others because he'd been slightly distracted by the excitement of his imminent trip to Australia. With a bit of luck, there might even be something there that wasn't complicated or controversial and which they might talk about at some point.

She pressed the button to play the tape and had to brace herself on hearing his voice, which almost immediately plunged into talk of death and suicide pacts, but in an incoherent and rambling way so that she very quickly couldn't make head or tail of it and after only a couple of minutes she pressed the stop button and sat as still as a statue, her heart hammering against her chest. She'd already begged him numerous times to be upbeat and not talk about all those things, but to no effect. Perhaps his condition really did mean that he was unable to consider the feelings of other people, so perhaps she shouldn't hold it against him, but it did seem so unfair to off-load it all onto her. Had things been different, she might even have confided in him about her own life, but there was obviously no chance of that happening.

It wasn't that she was unhappy now—she really wasn't—and she was just trying to decide what she really *would* like to talk to Murray about if there were no barriers, when the doorbell rang and her heart leapt in alarm. Quickly she bundled the letters away into a draw, took a deep breath and went to answer it.

She almost did a double take on opening the door when she saw him standing there in front of her, so tall, tanned and handsome. She hadn't seen any photos of him for a long time—in fact the last ones were probably from when he'd passed out at Sandhurst 12 years ago. Practically a lifetime.

Her eyes filled with tears as she hugged him and he, too, seemed moved to be together again. Or at least, he allowed her to hang on to him, which was a damn sight more than anyone else had done for a very long time.

'Nice place you've got here, Miriam,' he said as they passed through the front door and into the hallway.

She beamed. 'Well, it's less cramped than the VW, but what a *lucky* find that was, Murray, and you've done wonderfully well with it, travelling simply thousands of miles and I'm *dying* to hear about it all.

He was right about the house—she'd been very fortunate in that a friend of a friend's parents were upsizing, so they'd managed without any agency fees, plus she'd bought in 1972 when house prices were much more affordable than they were now. It was small—only two bedroomed—but very pretty and the garden was lovely, the crowning glory being a terrace which stretched the whole length of the back of the house.

It was to this delectable terrace that she now led Murray, keeping hold of his hand as if she might lose him along the way and after settling him in one of the cane chairs—fortunately cushioned—she instructed him not to go anywhere and shot off back into the house to make a pot of tea, thankful that should he be minded to hurl a tea cup anywhere, the garden would be the most obvious target.

Murray stretched and looked over his shoulder at the purply-pink bougainvillea which covered the back wall of the house and extended into the garden, where it had completely covered a wooden pergola. He'd travelled thousands of miles in the last few months—not to mention all the huge distances in India—so this was the end of a very long trip for him and he had to admit that he was physically quite tired. It would be good to be back again in his little flat in Du Kane Court, but he could see why Miriam was so happy here and particularly in this little house, which really was a gem and in a very quiet suburb.

She returned in a very short time and he was pleased to note that she'd given them mugs, rather than the obligatory tea cups to which the rest of the family seemed committed.

'I remembered, you see?' she teased him as she poured out the brew and cut him a slice of fruit cake. 'My own make, so don't dare say anything rude about it,' she warned him, making a face.

Once they were both eating and drinking she continued, 'Well, I know next to nothing of where you've been since Darwin, so *do* tell. I imagine it's all the places which I should have been to and never have, so I'll just have to live with the shame.'

'Lovely cake, Miriam. I hope you're not expecting to have any left,' he responded.

'If it makes your travels sound sufficiently amazing, you can finish the lot, darling,' she told him, not entirely seriously.

Murray helped himself to a second slice and described his drive from Darwin to Alice Springs—the barren, central point in Australia—and his journey from there to the massive *Ayer's Rock* at Uluru. At that point he'd parked the VW and taken advantage of his free return flight to Perth and he filled Miriam in on the government's generous offer to all those who had mucked-in with the emergency repairs—first rate pay, two weeks holiday *and* free inland flights.

Fortified by the tranquillity and beautiful, white beaches around Perth, he'd caught a flight back to Uluru and driven the largest single leg of his travels—north-west to Cairns and the *Great Barrier Reef*, where he'd gone out in a boat snorkelling and viewed all the underwater wonders first hand. From there it had been south to the Gold Coast and then the last leg of the journey, taking in Melbourn, Frankston and now Sydney.

Miriam had tears in her eyes by the time he'd finished. 'Oh, I'm so ashamed! I've never been to *any* of those places and I've lived here 15 years!'

He was astonished, 'What, not *any* of them?!'

She blushed slightly. 'I know it's difficult to understand, but after travelling out here in the first place it was such a wonderful feeling of freedom that I never felt the need to travel outside of Sydney. Of course, I've been within a 30-mile radius or thereabouts because I've got a little car, but I just use it for day trips with friends and shopping...that sort of thing.'

'What about Frankston?'

Her voice quavered slightly. 'I haven't been. I'm sorry, Murray. I know I should have gone, but I don't think I could bear it and besides, it's a long way.'

Frankston was the little seaside town on the outskirts of Melbourn where they'd lived as ex-pats from 1942-45 during the War. It was about 550 miles from Sydney and had considerably grown in size since those early days, although more to the point was the fact that their mother was buried in the cemetery there.

'What's it like—the grave?' To her annoyance she could hear her voice faltering.

'A Celtic Cross in its own little square of turf. Quite pretty.'

'And the inscription?'

'*Taken too soon*...something along those lines.'

She was on the point of asking how he felt on seeing it and being in Frankston but stopped herself. Any family discussion with Murray—even going back as far as that—was dangerous territory. However, she noted that he didn't seem unduly moved by the experience, which perhaps wasn't surprising given that he'd only been a little over two years old when it happened and considered himself as being from another family in any case. What was perhaps more surprising was that he'd bothered to go there at all.

'Have you calculated how many miles you've driven?' she asked, anxious to change the subject now.

Without a shadow of embarrassment, Murray cut himself a third slice of cake. Well, actually it was quite easy to work out, because the camper van has done an additional 6,000 miles or so since I bought it, although the return flight to Perth was another 2,600 miles in terms of what I've *personally* travelled, although I confess I was asleep for most of it.'

'It's such a beautiful and diverse country. You must think there's something wrong with me, hiding away here for 15 years in the same place.'

Murray considered for a moment. 'I might if there wasn't a beach, but with *Bondi Beach* on your doorstep and others quite close, I don't think it's so very strange,' he reassured her.

She looked at him gratefully. 'Thank goodness for that. Anyway, I don't want to talk about me. What was your favourite part of the trip?'

He pondered the question for a moment. 'Well, snorkelling on the *Great Barrier Reef* comes pretty high up the list, but if I was going to live here I think I'd settle somewhere around Perth, because it's so unspoilt. Beautiful, empty beaches all around...but of course I haven't seen Sydney yet. I might change my mind.'

The prospect of Murray coming to live anywhere in the same country as her made Miriam's heart miss several beats. 'We can't compete with Perth in terms of being unspoilt, I'm afraid,' she said hurriedly, before continuing, 'Although of course it's very beautiful here and over the next few days I'll show you around. There's *Bondi Beach*, the opera house, the harbour bridge...you'll have to let me know if there's anywhere in particular that you want to go.'

He nodded and she added, 'We can actually drive across the bridge to the centre, if you like, although there's also a good bus service. Then from the harbour we could take any number of ferry rides. I believe Paramatta is a good one.' Miriam stopped short, feeling that she was beginning to gabble in her efforts to appear knowledgeable about her adopted country.

Murray leaned back and stretched his legs. 'Don't worry about me, darling. I'm quite happy to be led wherever you think best.'

Miriam smiled. 'Well, it's your party—so to speak—and please feel free to...' not being quite sure what she wanted to say, the sentence was never finished, but he didn't appear to notice.

It was beginning to sound a bit like a *Mutual Appreciation Society* and she wondered if he was thinking that it was all terribly insincere. She also found herself wishing that it wasn't school holiday time, because if for any reason this visit took a nosedive—which was more than possible—there would be nowhere for her to run to.

* * * * * * * * * * * *

They were five days in and it had actually gone terribly well, all things considered. Miriam was so relieved that she could almost have wept, although

Murray still hadn't said how long he was staying and she was fearful of asking in case he took offence and everything went down the tube, because she knew from what Marjorie and Josephine had said that his mood could change in an instant at the least little thing.

Another problem was that he hadn't offered to give her anything towards his keep and he was eating like a horse, although all things considered, that was a small price to pay for a smooth ride. Besides, who knew when they might meet again, if ever?

They'd already visited most of the tourist hot spots, starting off with a two-hour ferry trip to the old Colonial city of Parramatta, then endless walking around the harbour area where he'd surprised her by buying a soft toy platypus which he insisted was only for good luck. They'd also walked around the outside of the *Opera House*, but agreed that at £3.50 each it was far too expensive to go inside. She'd even driven him an hour inland to the *Blue Mountains,* where they'd stood on a little ridge and gazed across the dividing chasm at the ancient trio of rocks, named after three Aboriginal sisters. Legend had it that they'd fallen in love with three brothers, but tribal law had forbidden them to marry.

Murray hadn't mentioned the family at all and neither had she. Instead, he'd talked a lot about his travels in India and Australia, telling her little anecdotes along the way to make her laugh. In a way it also made her want to weep, because this was so much the *old* Murray that she'd grown up with. At times the fanciful side of her had even managed to blot out the existence of his frightful alter-ego, but never for very long because she knew only too well that it *did* exist and those awful tapes were testament to that, not to mention the experiences of the rest of the family.

She made a point of sounding him out about the places on his travels which had been worth a visit and those that weren't, as she really would have loved to go on a trip like that with the right person, although now she almost certainly never would. It was just a pipedream really, given that she was committed to remaining single and besides, if she was honest she'd received no male interest anyway since that second break up. Miriam had a theory that she gave off a certain vibe which acted as a deterrent to single males and although in a way that was good, it was also a bit of a pity when she was still only in her late 30s. Still, there it was—for better or worse she was done with the mating game.

It really would take being in a relationship for her to do the kind of trip that Murray had done, because it would be too lonely to go on her own—even if she had the nerve—and all her friends were married or with children now. Not to mention that she'd need quite a lot of money, plus time off work which they almost certainly wouldn't give her. No—the very idea was completely impractical.

On impulse she asked Murray how much he was hoping to get for the VW—but without letting on that she might be interested—and he said around £750 in English money which sounded pretty steep, although she could have afforded it at a push. However, for as long as she was still working it really was just a dream and she pushed it to the back of her mind.

The one thing they hadn't done yet was to go and see the celebrated *Carthona* on *Darling Point,* a house which had been built and once owned by their great grandfather Sir Thomas Mitchell. He'd been surveyor general of New South Wales from 1827 in the very early days of the colony until his death in 1855 and had made quite a name for himself in government, largely because successive governors hadn't spared themselves in their efforts to get rid of this turbulent servant of the crown—a task which was to take them nearly 30 years.

Their zeal in seeking his dismissal had in no degree been due to a lack of ability—on the contrary he was overflowing with it—but was almost entirely on account of his indifference to authority and an extremely warm temper. Nevertheless, countless roads, bridges and towns remained as a testament to his brilliance and many of them were named after him. There was even a *Major Mitchell Cockatoo*—now critically endangered—resplendent in beautiful salmon pink and crowned with an astonishing dark pink and gold headdress.

However, Sir Thomas hadn't been able to swim against the tide forever and eventually the enemies he'd made along the way succeeded in their endeavours to the point that at the age of 63 he'd been left high and dry with insurmountable debts and negative equity on a string of properties.

Events were just gearing up for an ignominious end in the bankruptcy courts when—resourceful to the end—Sir Thomas had confounded his enemies by unexpectedly dying of pneumonia, forcing the incumbent governor to hastily withdraw the proposals for his imminent dismissal and fork out for a state funeral instead.

Miriam looked over at Murray, who was in his habitual pose whenever they sat on the terrace: reclining with his legs outstretched and his eyes closed. Any concerns that she might have had about him not settling in couldn't have been further from the truth and if anything the opposite was true and he was making himself a little *too* much at home.

With an effort she injected a note of brightness into her voice and asked, 'Shall we go and see great grandfather's place at *Darling Point* tomorrow? It's really not very far.'

'All right, anything you say.'

It wasn't exactly the response she'd been looking for and Miriam felt rather annoyed. He could surely show a bit more interest and even gratitude at the effort she was making on his behalf. However, Aunt Marjorie had already made it clear that Murray wasn't big on gratitude.

However, Sir Thomas was a celebrated historical figure in Australia and his importance far exceeded the bounds of anything to do with the family. He'd been one of those very rare characters whose genius spanned several genres, from engineering to fine art, poetry, languages, science, mathematics and even invention, although it was in exploration that he'd made his name. In fact, it was his frequent absences in one or other wilderness for up to two years or so at a time which had caused some of his most serious run-ins with those in authority.

Miriam had been bemused to discover that a little used expression of 'doing a Major Mitchell' was in the dictionary as a reference to wandering around looking lost, which she supposed he must have done quite a lot of, although his brilliant maps were works of art which had subsequently become very valuable.

She now repeated the 'doing a Major Mitchell' anecdote to Murray, hoping to elicit a flicker of interest if nothing else, but he simply said, 'Well, he's not my family, so you can't expect me to feel about it as you do.'

So there it was. Perhaps she was lucky that they'd got as far as five days before he'd brought it up. However, she circumvented this provocation with the observation that as Sir Thomas was a national figure, it really had very little to do with the family if he didn't want it to.

Having put this point across and been rewarded with a deafening silence she finally said, 'Well, unless you've got any ideas for something you'd *rather* do, I think it would be lovely to go for a walk at Darling Point tomorrow and we might as well look at the house while we're there—at least from the outside.'

Again, Murray didn't reply and she was just about to escape to the kitchen and start cooking supper when he said suddenly, 'I'd been seeing quite a lot of Frank before I came away.'

The name didn't register with her and she frowned slightly. 'Frank who?'

He opened his eyes at that and she laughed. 'Well, at least *that* got a reaction.'

'Frank your *brother*,' he said, in a tone heavy with sarcasm.

She paled. 'I thought he was dead.'

Murray looked at her incredulously. 'Why would he be dead?'

Miriam felt suddenly very awkward. 'Well, they—I mean what he had—they don't live very long, do they? He wasn't expected to live beyond the age of about 12.'

'Don't you think the family would have let you know if he'd died?'

'I suppose I just assumed that they hadn't got around to letting me know, but to be completely honest, I hadn't really thought about it.'

He stared at her in a way which made her feel extremely uncomfortable. 'Well, I'm sure *the family* would have found it much more convenient if he *had* died.'

She felt tears in her eyes. Something dreadful was going to happen, she was sure of it. 'But Frank had—or has—a very poor quality of life. Can the family be blamed if we *did* feel that he'd be better off dead?'

'Well, you could at least have spared him a thought in all these years instead of inexplicably assuming that he was dead.'

Miriam couldn't have said why it was that she'd put Frank's existence completely behind her. Perhaps the fact that no family letters ever mentioned him had had something to do with it, but it did open up a moral question for her that she absolutely didn't feel equipped to deal with, just now.

'But you didn't think of *anybody* else when you left, did you?' he said, changing tack slightly, and not to her advantage.

She looked away from him and addressed the bougainvillea extending out from the terrace to the garden. 'Who should I have thought of?'

She'd always known that it was going to come to this at some stage, because it had already come out in those damned tapes and if it meant that now they were going to have a big row, perhaps it was for the best and she could get rid of him. He was absolutely on the attack now and if there was going to be a big scene, please God, let it happen now.

He stared at her sullenly. 'Well, me for one.'

'When I left, you were already a grown man at *Sandhurst* and doing *very* well with a life of your own. And quite besides that, why should I ask your permission for anything? You're not my keeper and I certainly wouldn't *dream* of trying to stop *you* from going anywhere you wanted to.'

'You were being selfish, just running away and thinking only of yourself. Pretending Frank never existed and completely forgetting about me.'

Miriam did feel guilty about Frank, but it wasn't that she hadn't cared about him. On the contrary it was because she'd never wish that sort of life on anyone and somehow fantasy and reality had collided and he'd become dead to her. How else could she explain it? Being separated by thousands of miles probably had something to do with it, but she couldn't even begin to put it into words.

'What's Frank like now?' she asked, hoping to deflect his hostility.

'Very affectionate, loves cars and especially mine, because it's yellow. A bit overweight now, though, and going bald. Thinks his mother was a film star because I said she liked drama, so I haven't disavowed him of the fantasy.'

Miriam's felt tears on her cheeks for the tragedy that had been Frank's: his limitations, then being cut off from the rest of the family and going into a home when he was probably only 4 or 5 years old. She wondered how much he understood of what had happened to him or realised that other people had families. She felt fairly certain that no one in the family had seen him for several years—apart from Murray, apparently—or she'd have heard about it.

Was he still angry with her? It was hard to tell. 'What do you do together when you see him?' she asked, eventually.

'Walking on the beach, going in those little shops on the promenade, taking him for rides around Hove and to other places. We went to *Beachy Head* once. Often we share a packet of chips on the beach.'

She had a sense that Frank had become important to him and guessed that he hadn't told anyone in the family about it or they would certainly passed it on and as if on cue he interrupted her train of thought with, 'Naturally I haven't told any of *them*. They'd only try and put a spanner in the works if I did.'

She didn't contradict him, although she doubted that he was correct—on the contrary the family would probably be delighted that one of their number had taken on a responsibility which they themselves should never have relinquished. To all intents and appearances it did seem that they'd abandoned Frank to his fate and she wondered why, because surely they must know that he was still alive.

'I think you're doing a marvellous thing, Murray, and I'm so glad that you've found each other,' she said finally.

He looked at her sharply. 'I get just as much out of it as he does, possibly even more. I'm not doing him any favours—he's good company and we have a really good time together.'

'Yes, I understand that,' she said, hurriedly, and then after a moment added, 'I do agree with you that the rest of the family—myself included—have behaved very badly in neglecting him as we have.'

Feeling slightly disorientated she got up a little too quickly, her chair scraping the tiled floor. Dinner now seemed long overdue. 'How does *chilli con carne* sound?' she asked, forcing herself to sound upbeat, but he didn't reply and she hurried through to the kitchen.

The rest of that evening was subdued but passed without incident and they both retired to bed early, Miriam desperately hoping for a reprieve from what might be a heavy dose of reproach the next day and her worst fears came true as she stood staring up at the Gothic manor house of *Carthona*. With its warm-coloured sandstone, slate roof, ornamental arches and carved stone heads it was very easy on the eye, but that didn't translate to her state of mind.

She'd been before at least twice—living so close it would have been difficult not to have done—but each time she felt the same sense of pride. He'd been a great man in many ways, although they'd been a strange and tragic family, with none of his 12 children reaching the same heady heights of fame as their father. On the contrary, most of them had singularly failed in one way or another and had mostly died young either through accident or illness, although fortunately for Sir Thomas most of that had happened after his own death and it had been poor Lady Mitchell who lived into her 80s and suffered the fate of seeing eight of her adult children dropping around her like flies, not forgetting another who'd died as a child in undocumented circumstances.

They'd become a singularly dysfunctional family, rather like Miriam's own, what with her mother, father and both brothers variously slapped down either by fate or their own bad judgement—and sometimes both.

Murray was refusing to be interested in *Carthona* and rather than afford the house even a cursory glance, he made a show of walking slowly and aimlessly down the street, whistling to himself.

She sighed, wishing that he could simply appreciate a beautiful house for what it was, instead of obsessing about a family connection which he didn't feel part of.

She hurried to catch up with him. 'Did you see the carved stone heads on the arches?' she asked him, knowing very well that he hadn't, because he hadn't looked at the house at all.

He ignored her and she continued, 'He carved them himself with faces of his friends. They say that they're all over the house. Mind you, he must have done some of his enemies as well because there's some of the governors among them.'

She felt very miserable and wished again that Murray would just go away and never come back. She'd shown him everything that she could think of in and around Sydney and sat by for nearly a week now while he ate her out of house and home, yet he was repaying her by being as unpleasant as possible. Naturally, she was aware that he could be a lot worse than this and decided that it was now or never—she had to speak openly and wrap things up before it got to that stage.

He'd still given no indication at all of when he planned to leave and on impulse she asked him if he'd booked his ticket home yet.

'Why, are you trying to get rid of me?'

This was the answer she'd been expecting and luckily it gave her the platform she needed. It didn't come naturally to her to speak so plainly, but there was a lot at stake and she simply had to go for it. 'We've had a lovely time, Murray and I've enjoyed it, but last night something changed and I think we should quit while we're ahead, so that we can part friends.'

It was a bravery born of desperation, but Murray responded with a slow hand clap which was in no sense intended to be congratulatory. 'Bravo, Miriam, Bravo.'

She flushed, but if anything his insolence only inflamed her further. 'You see what I mean? I'm sorry, Murray, but we've both changed too much in the last 15 years and when you're like this, you scare me.'

'Are you scared of me now, Miriam?'

'Yes.'

He reflected on this for a few moments and then said matter-of-factly, 'Well then, I'd better go.'

Relief and sorrow washed over her in equal measure. 'I wish it wasn't like this, I really do.'

They turned and walked back towards where the car was parked. Had things not taken a turn for the worse she'd been going to suggest that they hire a rowing boat and view *Carthona* from the harbour. It was something that she'd never done before and it was such a pity that instead of cementing their reunion, it had come to this. They walked to the car in silence and as she started the engine he said, 'It's just as well that you're not my real sister. I've known that you were an imposter for as long as I can remember, but didn't want to upset you by saying so.'

She felt cold inside and crunched the gears in her confusion, although it hardly came as a surprise. 'Whatever you say, Murray.'

'Lies always catch up with you,' he persisted. 'I put up with it because despite everything I liked you, but I suppose it doesn't matter now that we've got separate lives.'

The 15-minute journey home seemed interminable and before he got out of the car she said, 'If you could pack as soon as possible I'd be grateful. Actually, make that straight away. I'll give you some food to take.'

'Don't bother, I'd probably choke on it,' he spat back and she felt her heart harden. He certainly had a damnable cheek criticising her food when he'd spent so much of this past week eating as much of it as possible.

It was as she asked. In less than ten minutes he'd packed his black, metal trunk—severely dented now after the efforts of *Cyclone Tracey*—and walked out of the front door without another word or even a glance in her direction. Thankfully she watched out of the window as he drove down the road and breathed a sigh of relief as the VW disappeared from sight. There were plenty of places he could park in the suburbs and as long as she didn't have to see him again, anywhere was fine with her.

It was certainly just as well that she'd decided against buying the camper van, because the way things had gone, there was certainly no way she'd have ended up with it.

Mechanically she made a mug of tea and walked through to the terrace where Bella eyed her appraisingly from the dog bed which nestled in one corner under the shade of the purple bougainvillea. She and Murray had spent so many happy hours here before it all went wrong, yet with hindsight she thanked her lucky stars that they'd got as many as five good days and that she hadn't allowed the downturn to drag on.

Putting the mug to her lips she took a sip and wondered why the hot liquid made her body feel so cold. Perhaps it was something to do with knowing that she'd never see him again and indecision as to whether that made her feel wholly dead or partly alive.

Calypso sauntered onto the terrace and jumped on her lap, in his own way conveying to her the answer. Of course, she didn't need Murray—or want him for that matter. That part of her life was over, just like her relationships with the married men. Why was it always men who brought strife and grief? Calypso and Bella were more than enough for her and she didn't want it any other way.

Chapter 7

September 1975
Du Kane Court, London

It had taken Murray a long time to calm down after his abrupt departure from Miriam. Barely aware of where he was going, he'd driven blindly and ended up in the northern suburbs of Sydney where he mooched around for another six days before catching a flight home. In fact, he'd pre-booked it months earlier but hadn't wanted to give her the satisfaction of knowing that, because she'd so obviously wanted to get rid of him. She'd clearly been *dying* to ask, but it had suited him to force her hand and he was mildly impressed that she'd held back so long.

It was typical of the way his so-called family behaved, saying one thing and thinking another, so that you never knew where you were with them. He actually thanked God that he wasn't related by blood to any of them or he really *would* have started worrying about his own sanity. All the same, it brought into sharper focus the pervading issue of his true origins, as he'd now reached the end of the line with all but his cousins Triss and Evie, the only trouble being that he'd never known them very well in the first place.

The question of his future seemed an insurmountable dead end and his last days in Sydney had been so dark that it was as if the many joys of his year-long trip had simply been blotted out. In fact, given his state of mind it was perhaps fortunate that he arrived back in England to such a cascade of domestic chaos that it catapulted him into survival mode, necessarily forcing issues of betrayal and identity to take a back seat.

The first shock was that the bloody lodger had left without his knowledge several months earlier, leaving the flat in a mess, a hefty rent shortfall and a deluge of final demands which liberally covered his doormat. And given that the record player was inexplicably missing, he could only assume that as a final two fingered gesture, she'd made off with that as well.

Once Murray had recovered sufficiently to sit down and meticulously go through it all, it transpired that mortgage and bills collectively amounted to over £550, with the largest single bill ironically coming from *British Telecom,* whose eye-watering demands had their origins in several lengthy international phone calls to Argentina. It was just as well that the culprit had done a bunk or he'd have bloody killed her.

Brimming over with fury and indignation, Murray watched helplessly as most of the £650 he'd finally managed to salvage on the camper van was swallowed up in debts and was so unnerved that he even went to see his bank manager. With an empty bank account and roughly £100 in cash to his name, it was an understatement to say that the future looked daunting, not to mention that the next mortgage payment would be upon him before he knew it.

Sadly, the bank manager wasn't at all reassuring, his principle advice being to sell the flat as quickly as possible and get something smaller and in a less prestigious area. He even had the nerve to suggest that Murray put himself on the Council housing list. However, the crunch came when he declared that having the *Triumph Herald* was also unnecessarily flamboyant and selling it would give him some capital, not to mention money saved on petrol, tax and insurance. Murray responded unequivocally that he'd rather slit his own throat and this had the effect of bringing their conversation to an abrupt close.

To add to his miseries, the housing slump that had engulfed the whole country was at its height and it was the worst possible time to sell. His beautiful flat wasn't worth much more than the £4,000 or so that he'd paid back in 1966—a whole nine years ago—and most of that would go on repaying what he still owed, interest, cancellation fees and God knew what else. They really knew how to bleed a chap dry.

The perverse irony of someone like himself—brilliant and well-connected—being forced into a position of such shame and humiliation very nearly overwhelmed him, to the point that he could only function mechanically.

However, the machinations of penury had already creaked into gear unbidden and Murray had no choice but to fall on his sword.

The first consideration was his flat, which he put on the market with *Knight, Frank & Rutley* simply because they were the most prestigious name he knew of in the mire of the estate agency world. The lady agent who took all the details, made a strong case for supplying the agency with their own key so that they could show people around in his absence and after considerable soul-searching he conceded on the basis that being forced to watch commoners haggling over his property would be intolerable and his absence would be preferable to all concerned. Besides, there was nothing in the flat worth stealing except for his record collection, which was somewhat superfluous now that he had no record player. Thankfully it hadn't been a particularly valuable one, but that was hardly the point.

After forcing himself through the doorway of the Knightsbridge estate agents, he spent the next few days queueing for hours in Fulham's singularly unprepossessing dole office, submitted himself to an interview with a complete moron at the adjoining *Job Centre*, scoured the *London Standard* for jobs and presented himself before a debt counsellor at the *Citizen's Advice Bureau* regarding his household bills. He even went to Chelsea's *Council Offices* to put himself on the housing list, as although he didn't have the slightest intention of degrading himself to such an extent, it calmed him to know that he was covering all eventualities.

He couldn't even go and see Frank because he had no petrol and in any case, the car wasn't in working order after being left standing for a year.

Having lied to the man at the dole office and claimed that he didn't even have money for food, Murray was provided with an emergency payment of £25 which had to last him for the next two weeks until his application kicked in, following which he'd receive £17 a week.

Unemployment was the highest it had been since the War and he cursed the irony of his downturn in fortune occurring—completely coincidentally—at exactly the wrong time. After all, his personal circumstances were entirely the result of having been away for a year, yet if it had been *any* other year in recent history there would have been *no* recession, *no* unemployment and everything would have been all right.

He walked round to the Fulham office of the courier company where he'd previously worked but there was nothing currently available and he agreed to call in every week to check the situation. Ideally he would have left his telephone number, but had arrived back just too late to avoid the line being cut off and was still waiting for all that to be sorted out. However, he left his address and the company agreed to drop a note round if anything came up at short notice.

All told, the week which followed his return was one of unimaginable personal turbulence, to the point that he sometimes couldn't even remember where he was. It was an added complication which he could have done without and happened for the first time after the interview with his bank manager, when he was still reeling from the unspeakable horror of losing his flat. Other people had families to bail them out—as Marjorie was currently doing with Tristan—but for Murray there was no one.

He was used to not knowing *who* he was—he'd lived with that nearly all his life—but this new amnesia was something quite different and he attributed it to powerful, dark forces who were almost certainly in league with his father.

The first couple of times it happened he simply found a place to sit down and waited for five or ten minutes until his mind cleared, but then had the idea of writing down his intended movements at the beginning of each day before leaving the house and keeping the list in his pocket, so effectively speeding up the memory processes and generally managing to recover his wits within a minute or so.

This was the first of two new and unwelcome developments which occurred in the upheaval following his return and the second happened when he was taking a short cut home across Holland Park and to his utter amazement saw a mirror image of himself walking towards him quite nonchalantly, without a care in the world. He was even dressed in the same clothes and walked straight past without any acknowledgement or even a glance at Murray, who stared in amazement, willing the vision to meet his eye.

When they drew level the man was so close that they could almost have touched, but at that point he seemed to disappear, melting into the ether as if a thick fog had descended into the space where the creature had been.

Murray had an idea that there was a name for this sort of phenomenon and rushed home to consult his dictionary and Thesaurus. He found the word all right—doppelganger—whose definition was: *a biologically unrelated lookalike or double of a living person*. It was also described as a ghostly or paranormal phenomenon and usually a harbinger of bad luck.

The definition left him even more appalled and confused than he'd been before. With all the difficulties which had beset him since his return, Murray had barely taken any notice of the goons, although several times he'd been aware that they were there, spying on him as usual. Now, however, it was clear that the campaign against him had been stepped up—hence his amnesia and the doppelganger.

He wondered if his periods of amnesia, confusion and disarray were caused by the doppelganger attempting to merge its paranormal self with the real Murray and if so, was he in danger? He couldn't decide where it was all leading and to his great frustration only ever came up with more questions than answers. However, one thing which he always came back to was that he'd quickly learned to foil the amnesia with physical plans and lists and that was a huge step forward.

It wasn't the first time that he'd outwitted his enemies with brilliance and resourcefulness, but something told him that the stakes were getting higher and he spent long hours mulling over who was behind it and whether it was malevolent, or just a distraction or something else entirely?

The doppelganger hadn't been following him, but actually walking in the opposite direction. Did that mean something in itself? It had also seemed very carefree—quite the opposite to the real Murray—and was it capable of speech? He determined to try and talk to it if he saw it again and sat for hours in his flat, pondering different outcomes and never coming to any conclusions. Disconcertingly the creature had looked physically rather better than Murray did himself, almost like a super-power version—purposeful and self-assured.

He didn't experience it again for several days, but when it did happen, the experience was almost more bizarre than before. It happened just after another unsuccessful visit to the *Job Centre* and as he was returning along the Waterford Road he happened to glance into the window of a coffee shop and was dumbstruck to see the doppelganger sitting on a bar stool in the window, drinking something and apparently reading *The Spectator*—a magazine which Murray had never read in his life.

He stopped and stared. It wasn't dressed in the clothes which Murray was wearing that day, but in clothes which he did actually possess and it didn't look up, apparently blissfully unaware of being the object of his attention. He stayed for several minutes just staring, but decided against engaging with the thing because any degree of recognition was beneath him and might even be dangerous.

It had been a curious sensation seeing himself as others saw him, rather than the mirror image to which humanity was generally restricted, but even so he was annoyed with himself for spending all those minutes staring at it. That mustn't happen again and in the meantime he'd have to apply himself to researching the theories surrounding these creatures. Forewarned was forearmed.

Thus it was that he found himself at *Chelsea Library* in the *Old Town Hall* in Kings Road, where his initial approach was to consult encyclopaedias, but despite spending over an hour perusing various books, he learned nothing new and would have felt a rising tide of frustration, had it not been for the unexpectedly calming influence of the library itself.

There was something about the books and the meticulous manner in which they were categorised that he found very therapeutic and on discovering that membership was free, he spent some minutes at the desk filling in his details on the obligatory white postcard. It was annoying that both address and telephone number would almost certainly be changing in the near future and he'd then have to go through it all again, but that couldn't be helped. Moreover, his telephone line wasn't even re-connected yet, although he doubted that the Library would have reason to call him any time soon.

Would the doppelganger and the goons follow him to his new abode or start harassing him in other ways? Murray seemed to have no idea about anything anymore, but instinctively felt that the library was a place of refuge where he'd be safe. Suddenly he felt very tired, beset on every side by problems of such magnitude that he could barely begin to assimilate them.

On impulse he decided to go for a long walk along the river, having nothing to do at home, no job to go to, no money to get his car back on the road and no way of getting down to Hove again in the foreseeable future. He wondered if Frank would even remember him after all this time, given that it was over a year since they'd last met.

He was heading south along the King's Road towards the river when he noticed a record shop and instinctively went inside, spurred by the window display of the new *Pink Floyd* album, *Wish You Were Here*. He'd never taken much notice of *Pink Floyd* until their album, *Dark Side of the Moon*, which had pretty much set a new bar in rock music. He'd taken the cassette with him on holiday and played it endlessly in the VW until the bloody tape deck had chewed it up beyond all hope of salvage. Probably he'd simply played it too often, as all his less prized cassettes had annoyingly survived unmolested.

Now he couldn't even afford to replace what he'd lost, let alone buy the latest one. Nevertheless, he voluntarily tortured himself by leafing through the *Pink Floyd* section, lingering over the two coveted albums. The *Dark Side of the Moon* cover with its already iconic triangular prism on a black background and *Wish You Were Here* looked as if it might become equally celebrated, with its image of two white-suited men calmly shaking hands in the middle of a wide street, one of them with flames licking at the entire rear part of his body from head to foot.

In the old days, Murray would have bought both the vinyl and tape versions without a second thought, but now...

He was already back in the street when he felt a movement behind him and on turning around, saw a man whom he vaguely recognised as having been present in the shop. 'I believe you've got some goods that aren't paid for,' the man said, impassively.

'What?!' Murray was genuinely affronted.

'In your coat pocket,' the man prompted him.

He felt in his pockets and as if in a dream extracted the two coveted cassette tapes, staring at them helplessly.

'I don't know how they got there,' he heard himself say, uncharacteristically flustered and knowing that the words sounded trite and futile. Of course, nobody would believe him.

All the same, it was true—he *really* didn't know, and this wasn't the first time it had happened since his arrival back in England, although previously this uncharacteristic pilfering had been limited to odd bits of food and he'd never been caught.

The man didn't say anything, but gestured to him to go back into the shop, following which began a process which revealed to him that although he'd thought things couldn't get any worse, they most definitely could.

He was led to a back room and forced to wait while the Police were called, following which he was driven to Kings Road *Police Station* which was just a stone's throw away and all his personal details taken, along with fingerprints. He explained repeatedly that although it was true that he'd wanted to buy both tapes, he had no memory whatsoever of taking them. However, no one paid any heed and in the end he was told that he could leave and they'd be in touch.

Murray's heart was racing uncontrollably. 'Will I be charged?' he asked, feverishly.

The Officer was a languid individual in his late 50s and early retirement was looming. He shrugged, already largely oblivious to the petty criminal before him. 'We'll let you know. The CPS will make a decision once they've read the file and seen your medical report,' he informed him, indifferently.

This afforded Murray a glimmer of hope. He could tell the doctor about the doppelganger and that it must have been *him* who stole the tapes and then contrived for Murray to get the blame. He felt a surge of panic. Next time it might be something *worse* than shoplifting. What if the doppelganger *killed* someone? Murray might end up spending his whole life in prison for the crimes of a supernatural creature who was beyond human control!

He had no memory of getting home that afternoon, but somehow he did arrive and mechanically switched on the television, thankful that at least the electricity was still on. He'd had plenty of red bills from them, along with all the others, but the woman from the *Citizen's Advice Bureau* had done some sterling work in sorting things out and was still negotiating with *British Telecom* on his behalf for reinstatement of the telephone line. He was supposed to be going back to her office the next day for an update.

He didn't even know if the agents had brought anyone round to see the flat yet, because he was hardly ever in during the day and of course they couldn't phone him. He decided to call in there tomorrow and ask. It would at least create one small task to occupy him in the yawning cavern of a whole day to fill.

It was Children's TV time on BBC 1 and *Scooby Doo* was on, followed by *The Wacky Races* and *Hector's House*. He watched them wistfully, thinking of Frank and wishing that they could be enjoying these programmes together down in Hove, with Frank holding his hand and laughing. These days he frequently wondered if he'd ever laugh again.

Chapter 8

December 1975

When he looked back, Murray couldn't say for sure how he'd got through that period. Certainly, the woman at the *Citizens' Advice Bureau* had been admirable and the cooling corridors of the *Chelsea Library* had also provided him with a refuge, but one way or another things *did* work their way through to a series of conclusions which on the whole were the best outcomes that he could reasonably have hoped for.

Just five days after the unfortunate incident in the Kings Road record shop he'd received a letter from the *Crown Prosecution Service* requesting him to visit his own doctor in Chelsea for an assessment at a specified time, which he did. At the end of two hours during which the doctor resignedly spent a considerable time listening to theories about the goons and doppelgangers, he'd written a prescription and requested that Murray return the following week with a stern warning that if he didn't take the medication, then he would certainly end up in court.

Suitably cowed, Murray complied. One set of pills was anti-psychotic and the other for insomnia, the latter of which he'd suffered from on and off all his life, but it had become increasingly debilitating since his return from Australia.

A week later and the doctor seemed satisfied with the way that things were going and said he was going to recommend that on medical grounds the CPS *didn't* proceed. However, the recommendation would only stand if Murray underwent a three-month course of group therapy and if he didn't attend *every single* session in the proscribed period, then the prosecution would be reinstated. It came as such a relief that he almost wept.

The goons and the doppelganger didn't disappear, but they became noticeably less prevalent and Murray was in two minds as to whether he preferred this new state of affairs or not. After all, given that they *were* there, wasn't it better to be aware of them than not? However, fear of the consequences led him to obey the doctor's instructions with the result that he found himself free to concentrate on re-building his life.

The group therapy had been delayed until after Christmas, but Murray was glad about that, given that he already had so much else to contend with.

Thanks to the slump in the market there had so far been only two offers on the flat, but fortunately for him both buyers were keen and the best offer had risen to a heady £8,500—way above the initial asking price of £5,000.

After a long chat with his very resilient adviser in the *Citizen's Advice Bureau,* Murray finally conceded that if he was fortunate enough to be offered a Council flat then he ought to take it, given that the prices of private rentals in Chelsea and Fulham were way out of his reach. Moreover, a council property would not only be cheaper to rent, but probably bigger than anything he could afford on the private market, even in more downmarket areas. It was a stroke of luck that as he was living in Chelsea already, the Council was legally bound to re-house him there.

However, by the beginning of December the Council still hadn't contacted him with any offers and it wasn't until the *Citizen's Advice Bureau* got involved again that there was some movement. By mid-December he'd been offered a one-bedroom flat in a block called *Leastways* near the Kings Road and he went to view it with fear in his heart, knowing that to turn it down could get very awkward as he'd then be taken *off* the priority list and might not get any other offers at all.

However, much to his relief it wasn't as bad as he'd feared, being one of a relatively small complex of 30 flats in a quiet road where there was free parking—a rarity these days—although no garage for his precious Triumph Herald. However, the lady who showed him round said that there were some Council garages nearby and he might be able to rent one of those for £2 a week.

So, he agreed to take it and embarked on a mountain of paperwork which included a condition that he move in during the first week of January, 1976.

With very mixed feelings he reluctantly engaged a solicitor to go ahead with the sale of his flat and worked out that when all was said and done, he'd have something approaching £2,000 to put in the bank once everybody was paid off, plus his monthly rent would only be £25 a month—less than half of what his mortgage had been.

Obviously the flat wasn't *as* nice as *Du Kane Court,* but now that he'd got used to the idea of moving, he couldn't really have cared less about that. Not to mention that he had other fish to fry.

Murray's upward mobility from straitened circumstances was confirmed when his weekly visit to the courier firm paid off in mid-December with the news that someone had gone off sick and he could start immediately, with the position possibly to be made permanent. They even wanted him to start there and then, but he managed to put them off until the following day, by which time he'd managed to get his head together. It was curious how being out of work could take up the whole day, every day, and he wasn't completely sure that he'd ever manage to find the time to work again.

However, with a leap in his heart he realised that this would mean he'd be able to see Frank before Christmas and accordingly he arrived early for work the next day in order to plead for a pay advance so that he could get the *Triumph* fixed and buy petrol. It was touch and go and he had to plead his case very eloquently, but in the end the accounts clerk offered him a week's wages after one week's labour and honour was satisfied on both sides.

It felt amazing to be back at work, weaving around the roads and the traffic with the chill wind in his face. Everything was now illuminated for Christmas and there was an infectious excitement in the air which bolstered his mood. Murray didn't normally get excited about Christmas, but at the moment he was on a 'high' which didn't owe all its origins to medication. Sorting out the issues of flat and cashflow had done wonders for his self-esteem and in a way he was even glad to be leaving *Du Kane Court*, having spent so many fraught hours there being tormented by the goons. On principle he wouldn't have *chosen* to move to a council flat, but *Leastways* would do him for now.

His old ability to effortlessly negotiate the routes between banks hadn't deserted him, although he'd been a bit worried about it after his experiences with the amnesia. However, that, too, seemed to have eased off with the medication and nor had he seen any goons or doppelgangers for a few weeks now.

Murray arranged with a local garage to collect the *Triumph* and give it a service, with collection on December 23rd and then immersed himself in the routine of collection and delivery of bank documents all over London. Living a normal life again was like delivery from the jaws of Hell and he relished every moment.

The accounts department kept their word and paid him £55 as an advance on his monthly wage, enabling him to collect the car and still have plenty left over for petrol, food and a present for Frank. It was wonderful to be behind the wheel again and the first thing he did was drive to the Kings Road where he'd seen a little shop which sold Collectors' items, including Diecast model cars—if he could get hold of a yellow one, so much the better.

He parked in a side road and walked into the shop ten minutes before closing time. There were no longer any cars in the window but there were plenty inside and to his delight he saw an orange and white *VW Caravanette*, just like the one he'd had in Australia. He definitely had to have that one. There was also a lovely, dark green *Triumph Spitfire* and a yellow *Mini*. Perhaps he'd take all three and give Frank the choice of keeping two, with one for himself, then they could have races.

In the end it was decided for him when the owner said that there was a Christmas offer of 3 for 2. It cost him £4, but he couldn't have been happier. He thought that Frank would probably go for the brighter colours, leaving Murray with the *Spitfire*, which was in fact his favourite, so he'd be more than happy with that.

However, there was one other thing which he longed to do, if only he dared. Murray walked the short distance up to the record shop at no. 497 and stood outside, re-living his humiliation there—and not so long ago, either. *Wish You Were Here* was still resplendent in the window—evidently still sufficiently popular after three months to take the prime slot—so he walked into the shop and immediately saw the assistant who had challenged him over the 'stolen' tapes all those weeks ago.

The man moved towards him and taking a deep breath, Murray said, 'I've come to apologise. I was ill, you see, but I'm better now and thanks to what happened here, I've now got the medical attention I should have had a long time ago.'

The man nodded and smiled. 'As long as you're all right now.' He was tall and thin with a pale complexion and a worried expression. He reminded Murray a little of himself, ten years ago, except that *he'd* have been in an immaculate *11th Hussars* uniform rather than the scruffy, Rock n' Roll get-up of torn jeans and cheesecloth shirts. What on earth would the *Hussars* have made of *that*?

'Well, I'm getting there,' Murray corrected him, before adding, 'And there is something else...'

He walked out of the shop with a vinyl and cassette of each of the *Pink Floyd* albums, having expended the vast sum of £14. It was doubly extravagant, because what he should *really* have done was to buy a tape-to-tape recorder and made his own copies, so as to always have one at home and one in the car. It would also have been the first step towards duplicating all of his music in future without having to buy another record player.

However, he couldn't regret it. There was something about the feel of vinyl that he loved, plus you got the paraphernalia of stickers, the lyrics, the big picture on the cover... Cassette tapes didn't usually come with any of that, although of course they had their own advantages, such as being able to play them anywhere at all as long as you had a portable cassette deck with you.

He wasn't working now until December 27th—three whole days in which to see Frank, although maybe two days would be enough. The last thing he wanted was to overwhelm him with too much too soon.

Besides, he had the move coming up on January 4th and he'd probably need a whole day to pack what few possessions he had, not to mention that he needed a rest, so yes, he was sure that two days initially would be quite enough.

He started early the next morning, hardly able to wait before setting off because he was so anxious to re-play *Wish You Were Here* again, having played it right through in the car twice over the night before. He really would have to buy a cassette deck for the flat, but that would now have to wait until next month's pay packet.

It was exceptional, there was no doubt about it, but *Dark Side of the Moon* was still his favourite. The latest one was all about Syd Barrett, the founder band member who the others had chucked out when he'd got too wasted to play. He'd been the genius who'd got them to the place where they were today and Murray was in two minds as to whether giving the album that title and making several of the songs about him wasn't adding insult to injury—a marketing ploy to make even more money on the back of their tragic hero. The song, *Shine on you Crazy Diamond* was a masterpiece, but he couldn't help thinking that if he was Syd Barrett he'd feel like ramming it down their collective throats.

With an effort he focussed his mind on Frank, feverishly hoping that the long absence wouldn't count against him too much in terms of reestablishing their relationship. More to the point, would he even remember him?

Frank didn't really have a sense of time except for the here and now, but he very much had a sense of being happy or unhappy and Murray hoped that having known such happiness together wouldn't have resulted in withdrawal symptoms when the visits had stopped. It was something he wouldn't know until he saw him again.

He shouldn't really have had the hood down, but he couldn't resist it. The air was cool and clear but it was surprisingly mild for the time of year and there was no reason not to. The wind whipped his cheeks and his hair, *Shine on you Crazy Diamond* blared through the speakers and Murray felt positively happy for the first time since...when? There had been lots of good times on his travels and even with Miriam before it all went wrong, although he didn't want to think about her now—or anytime for that matter. He was done with her.

The bitch had even had the cheek to send him a Christmas card after all she'd said to him, but he'd sent it straight back to her and hoped that she'd have to pay the postage. No, he certainly didn't want to have to think of *her* on a day like this.

He leaned back in his seat and felt the wind streaming over him. Frank would love this. Suddenly he couldn't wait to get him in the car and share it all.

The door of the home was shut when he arrived just before 9 am, which wasn't surprising really, given that it was winter. He tried the door, expecting it to open and when it didn't he rang the bell and waited impatiently until a woman in nurse's uniform eventually came to the door. She was youngish with green eyes, golden hair swept up behind her cap and a tanned, heavily freckled face.

'I've come to take Frank out,' he said, feeling that the direct approach was best.

She looked surprised. 'Oh. I'm afraid he hasn't been at all well for some time now, but perhaps he'll be all right if we wrap him up warmly.'

As soon as she spoke he recognised that she was Australian which was rather a coincidence, but his plummeting spirits dispensed with any possibility of small talk. 'What's wrong with him?'

The nurse led him inside and they stood talking in the hallway. 'It started over a year ago. I can't put my finger on it, but he became depressed, didn't want to do anything—not even eat. You'll see that he's lost a lot of weight. Then he got a heavy cold which wouldn't shift. They have weak hearts, you know, with his condition, so any infection hits them hard.'

'Where is he?' Murray asked, wanting to rush to that place immediately, wherever it was.

The nurse looked at him curiously. 'He's in his room. He always stays there now, rather than go to the *Day Room*.'

'Can I go up?'

'Yes, I'll show you the way. It should cheer him up to have a visitor. I can't remember the last time he had one.'

They went up a wide, wooden staircase and Murray was reminded that pre-war, this would have been a rather grand, private house.

When the nurse opened the door of Frank's room, Murray did a double take. His brother had lost shedloads of weight and looked very pale, sitting up in bed in his pyjamas, reading a child's board book.

'Frank!' Murray couldn't even say any more than his name because he was so overwhelmed.

'Hello Murray,' Frank replied solemnly, evidently less overwhelmed.

'You remembered.'

'Of course I did. I'm not stupid.'

Murray rushed over and grasped the pale hand which lay on top of the bedclothes. 'I'm really sorry that I was away so long.'

At that point, much to his relief, the nurse turned and left the room with a cheery, 'Well, I'll leave you to it then,' but neither of them made any reply.

'I nearly died because of you,' Frank said, accusingly.

Murray was aghast. 'Why?!'

'Because you left me. You made me ill.'

Murray hugged him. 'I'm really sorry, Frank. I've been ill, too.'

'Good.'

'Why good?' Murray was beginning to realise that he had some ground to make up. Thank God Frank hadn't died.

'Because then you'll know what it's like.'

Murray took the rebuke without trying to defend himself. Frank hadn't smiled at him yet. 'I'm really, *really* sorry. I promise I won't do it again. I'll always be here for you.' He grasped a handkerchief out of his pocket and blew his nose noisily, then when he looked up again, Frank was smiling.

'It's all right, you don't have to cry. It might not have been *all* your fault.' Then, as Murray digested this, he asked, 'Have you still got the car?'

'Yes, we'll go in it when you're dressed, but in the meantime…' he brought out the three little cars which he'd bought the previous afternoon. Fortunately the man in the shop had gift-wrapped them, because Murray currently possessed neither paper nor Sellotape.

Frank took the package eagerly and randomly tore at the paper, which itself was adorned with a stylised print of old Austin 7s.

Murray winced, slightly. For himself he always took the utmost care in removing the paper undamaged, so that it could be re-used.

The three *Dinky* cars fell onto the bed one by one and a big smile creased Frank's face as he handled the boxes, peering at the cars inside.

'You can have them all if you like, or you can give me one and we'll have races on the beach. I can show you how to build a track with pebbles,' Murray offered, suddenly hesitant at the prospect of re-claiming one of the cars in case they were all coveted to the point of shared ownership being out of the question.

Frank considered for a moment and then picked up the orange and white *VW*. 'You can have this one.'

Murray was surprised. 'Well, that's very appropriate because I drove round Australia in one like that, so it will remind me of my holiday.'

Frank looked blank. 'Where's Australia?'

Murray shook his head. 'It doesn't matter. I'll tell you later.'

'I thought you said you'd been ill, not on holiday,' said Frank, unconcernedly admiring the green *Spitfire*, still currently in its box.

'I was ill in Australia,' Murray lied, by way of explanation and changing the subject asked, 'Do you like that one best?'

'Yes. It's my favourite colour and it's like your car.'

It transpired that a year in his sick bed had been sufficient time for reflection and Frank had made changes. Yellow was no longer his favourite colour, *Grange Hill* had replaced *Scooby Doo* as his favourite TV programme and he now liked *Abba*. He'd never mentioned pop music before and Murray envisaged a whole new world opening up before them. Feeling absurdly nervous he asked, 'Do you like The *Beatles*?'

'Yes.'

'Who else?'

'Elton John. That's all. Noone else.'

It was at least something to build on. 'How about I take you for a drive and play you a tape that I bought yesterday?'

'What's a tape?'

'It doesn't matter. I'll play you some new music and you can tell me what you think.'

Frank considered a moment. 'All right, but I want to open these first. Here, you take this one.' He pushed the *VW* into Murray's lap and started tearing clumsily at the cardboard which encased the *Triumph*.

'Look, if you open the lid you don't have to tear it and you can always keep the car in the box so that it stays nice and clean,' Murray explained, pointing to the appropriate folds.

Eventually all three cars were lined up on the bed and Frank clutched at his two, childlike, then lifting the *Triumph* he kissed it reverently, repeatedly, until Murray didn't know whether to laugh or cry.

'Why are you such a cry baby?' asked Frank, peeping at him over the roof of the *Spitfire*.

'I'm probably still a bit ill,' said Murray, dryly, wondering if Frank was being serious or if this was his sense of humour. He'd never exactly had a sense of humour before—or at least, not that he'd noticed—being simply like a child and with all the immediacy of a child, but little else.

'Oh, that's all right then,' Frank said.

It was strange, but somehow the long absence and their respective illnesses seemed to have given their relationship a depth that it hadn't had before. Murray felt that it was *absolutely* Frank who had changed and although he hated to say it, he looked a damned sight better for losing the weight.

Several minutes passed in admiring the cars and running them over Frank's rumpled bed clothes and then Murray held his clothes for him while he dressed himself in garments which had been neatly folded on the bedside chair, almost certainly *not* by Frank.

'New clothes,' Frank pointed out, which went without saying because he must be at least three sizes smaller now than he had been before and probably wasn't any heavier than Murray was himself, although he was a few inches shorter and his muscles were slacker. It also seemed an effort for him to bend down, but then he never got any exercise, so perhaps that was inevitable.

Despite being several sizes smaller than Frank's previous wardrobe, the clothes were similarly shapeless and obviously hand-me-downs. However, his denim jeans were fashionably faded and the shirt was bright orange and rather funky. 'I like this,' said Frank proudly, as he struggled to do up the buttons, then he looked over at Murray. 'Your clothes are boring.'

'Well, I've got some more interesting ones at home. I'll bring them next time,' said Murray, trying to keep a straight face. It was true that he generally wore quite boring clothes—*Citizen Smith* didn't generally go in for bright colours and Murray himself had never really caught on to the general exuberance of 1970s fashion, although he'd made an exception when on holiday in Australia and resolved to wear something more to Frank's taste the next day—if he even *wanted* a follow-up visit, of course.

They left the house without seeing anybody in the corridors and when Frank saw the *Herald* he ran towards it and leaned over the bonnet, stretching his arms out to either side as if giving it a hug.

'Come on,' Murray said eventually, impatient to be off. In truth, he was desperate to play *Dark Side of the Moon* to Frank, who now gave him a black look.

'I have to say hello. She's forgotten me because you stayed away so long.'

'She hasn't forgotten you.'

They both got into the car and Murray reversed out of the space. He hadn't mentioned the tape, but had purposely left it at the beginning of track 5 for maximum impact and because it began quietly, Frank didn't notice it at first. However, it wasn't long before an unearthly wailing was resonating like a melodic banshee and his mouth dropped open in astonishment.

'What *is* that?!'

'It's called, *The Great Gig in the Sky.*' Murray glanced sideways, trying to ascertain whether the question had been weighted with approbation or disapprobation.

'What, *that* sky?' Frank pointed up at the sky.

'Yes, that one.'

Frank listened, enraptured as the sound blasted out, enveloping them in something quite unique.

'It's a really small woman making that weird wailing sound. She was trying to make her voice sound as much as possible like a musical instrument and that was the result,' Murray explained, relieved that Frank seemed to have come down on the side of approbation.

'I love it,' he said, simply.

They drove without any further conversation, the wind carving their hair into pyramids and against all the odds injecting colour into both of their pallid faces.

It was 35 miles to Beachy Head and when they arrived some three quarters of an hour later, Murray parked in a small street not too far from the cliff edge, then walked along the wide, grassy promenade until they were standing almost in line with the famous red and white lighthouse. Rising up out of the sea nearly 200 yards from the base of the cliffs it seemed strangely prehistoric, like a benevolent monster with a giant, twinkling eye in the middle of its knobbly head.

'What *is* that?' Frank asked, staring at it in wonder.

'It's a lighthouse and it flashes a warning light, so that ships know to keep clear and don't get stuck on the rocks,' explained Murray.

'I can't see any rocks,' countered Frank, stubbornly.

'Well, there's probably some underwater, but even if there aren't, there's the cliffs here that we're standing on and they certainly wouldn't want to bump into *those* in the dark,' Murray replied, patiently.

It was like being with a child and having been the youngest all his life, dealing with a childhood sense of wonder wasn't something which Murray had ever experienced before. Even at school he'd always been the youngest in the class and it had never held him back. In fact, the opposite had been true, because if anything the glory had been magnified with each successive achievement on account of his extreme youth.

Keeping a respectful distance from the cliff edge, Murray sat down and fished the *VW Caravanette* out of his pocket. 'Where are yours?' he asked. It was a rhetorical question, but Frank nevertheless obliged and produced them from the pocket of an old tweed jacket—a garment of such establishment origins that it looked completely bizarre when twinned with the groovy orange shirt.

'I've got a jean jacket you can have, if you want,' Murray offered.

'All right,' Frank replied, oblivious to any necessity of gratitude.

Murray smiled. 'All right, I'll bring it tomorrow. You *would* like to see me on *Christmas Day*, I suppose?'

'Is it Christmas tomorrow?'

'Yes, and they've probably got a special meal for you at home. We'll have to check so that you don't accidentally miss it.'

He realised that strictly speaking, he should have said, *the* home, but it was quite a nice place really and somehow it didn't seem right to call it that. Frank clearly didn't get much attention beyond the provision of his basic needs, but what Murray had seen of the staff, they seemed quite nice and besides, short of actually sitting down and entertaining Frank all day, what *could* they do? It should be his family doing that side of things and once again he felt a burning anger that he'd just been dumped here and forgotten.

Miriam had mentioned in Australia that she knew Marjorie had seen Frank during the War when he was still very young and then post-war Murray and Miriam had been taken to see him maybe once or twice a year, but that must all have stopped at some point when they were teenagers in the mid-50s. It certainly looked as if Frank had been left on his own one way or the other for most of his life and specifically so for the last 20 years. Claude must be paying whatever it cost for the home, but that was it.

They lay flat on the grassy strip which spanned the promenade and spent over an hour carving out an impressive track in the sandy soil on which Murray built various obstacles, using his pen knife and bits and pieces from his pockets, including the torn *Dinky* box. Then, having perfected it to their satisfaction with ramps and bridges, they played on it for another hour or so until Frank asked, 'Can we come back here tomorrow?'

This seemed to be the cue to pack up and with that done, they crept a little closer to the cliff edge and peered over. Murray had heard that it was over 500 feet above sea level, although it didn't look anywhere near as much as that.

'If you drove the car off here, would it fly?'

Murray was startled by the question. It would at first if you drove off fast enough, but then it would crash into the sea.'

'Can we try it?'

There had been days recently when Murray might have taken him up on it, but he only said, 'Not today. If we did it, it would be the very last thing we ever did.'

Frank looked puzzled. 'What do you mean?'

'We'd die.'

'Oh, well that's all right then.'

Murray wasn't at all sure if Frank actually understood the concept of dying, but he said nothing and even Frank didn't pursue it as they walked slowly back to the car in silence.

Once they were back in the front seats of the *Triumph*, Murray asked, 'Shall we go back to Hove and get some chips?'

A big grin was all the answer he needed and it seemed a good sign that Frank's appetite had returned.

On the journey back to Hove, Murray played him *Wish You Were Here* for the first time and told him a little bit about the group's charismatic founder and now debunked member, Syd Barrett. Surprisingly Frank seemed quite curious. 'Why was he so ill?'

'He took some medicines which made him feel as if he was in another world which was better than this one.'

'So, what was wrong with that?'

'Well, nothing until he took too much and his body couldn't cope. Like when you eat too much, but worse.'

'Is he better now?'

'Not completely.'

From the little that Murray had read in *Rolling Stone* magazine, Syd was a long way from being completely better and never would be. He lived alone, but in what most people would describe as a state of chaos and one story doing the rounds had come from a delivery man who claimed that Syd had answered the door to him with what looked like a packet of flour tipped over his head.

Frank grinned widely when this story was recounted to him and Murray felt that it was just as well he didn't have access to the kitchens where he lived or there might have been some kind of a re-enactment.

However, he evidently liked this music and even turned up the volume of his own accord. Meanwhile Murray was more preoccupied with where he'd been this time last year—on the brink of one of the most momentous 24 hours of his life as *Cyclone Tracey* had homed in on Darwin. For most people it would absolutely have been the most momentous event in their lives, but in his case the helicopter crash which had nearly killed him definitely trumped it.

A strange sensation passed through him. It all seemed so very long ago and several lifetimes had passed since then.

Chapter 9

January 1976
Fulham Town Hall
Murray felt quite nervous, but he knew that he had to go in. There was absolutely no way out of it and besides, in a way part of him *wanted* to go because he didn't often get to talk to people socially and it could be quite lonely sometimes. Besides, he had to attend every single group therapy session for three months without fail or his shoplifting charge would be reinvoked. The group meeting was scheduled to start at 6 pm and would last for two hours, but other than that, he really didn't know what to expect at all.

When he walked through the doors it was 5.55 pm and he saw a cardboard sign with a black felt tip arrow at the back of the hall, pointing towards the right-hand side. This appeared to constitute the instructions, so he walked in the direction indicated and was about half-way down the hall when he heard footsteps behind him and on turning round, saw to his astonishment that a completely naked young man was striding in his wake at a rate of knots and would overtake him at any moment.

He appeared to be completely oblivious to his nakedness and once Murray had dragged his eyes away, he stared at the ground in some disarray. Having just thundered past him, the man then unexpectedly stopped short and asked peevishly, 'Well, are you coming, or not?!'

Murray felt like a rabbit in headlights. 'Yes', he muttered, still staring at the ground.

'Well, *get* a move on. They haven't got all day, you know!' And with that stern rebuke the man strode on swiftly in the direction of the arrow, only just about giving Murray time to take in his muscular body and curly, copper-coloured hair before he disappeared round the corner. He could almost have been some kind of fallen angel.

It turned out that Murray was the eighth arrival in the little back room, which helpfully had a paper sign reading 'Group Therapy' stapled over the doorway, just in case anybody was still in any doubt. As he sat down, the vision of nakedness was already being taken to task by a man who turned out to be the coordinator.

'Gideon, you've been *repeatedly* told to wear clothes when you come here!' he barked.

'I don't like clothes. I can't express myself in clothes.' Gideon was evidently used to holding his own on this topic and there was more than a note of sullen defiance in his tone.

The coordinator was a stout man in his 40s with receding hair and a moustache. With a sigh he held out a blue blanket. 'All right, put this round you, then.'

'No.'

The man glared at him, but it appeared that his initial, severe reprimand had been misleading for he now backed down like a lamb and instead turned his attention to Murray. 'And you are...?'

Murray told him and the man ticked off his name on a list, simultaneously introducing himself as Dennis. 'We're expecting three newcomers today, but you're the first to arrive. Hopefully you'll be able to tell us a little bit about yourself at some stage.' He smiled encouragingly.

Not counting Dennis, there were eight in the group so far and Murray thought that if he'd stuck everyone in the country into a lucky dip and drawn them out one by one, he couldn't possibly have picked a more random bunch of complete oddballs.

Opposite him was a tiny, wizened-looking woman with yellow, wrinkled skin, sharp features and black-rimmed glasses with thick lenses who was muttering to herself. She was so thin that she might have been anorexic and she wore a red and white triangular headscarf over most of her grey-streaked, greasy hair. She was dressed in shabby overalls with dirty jeans poking out of the bottom and—in no concession to the chilly, overcast evening—open-toed sandals.

Murray was just about to turn his attention to the others in the circle of seating when she suddenly leapt up and began an angry argument with herself, effortlessly adopting both roles and with each giving as good as they got, her voice echoing shrilly around the room.

'Oh, *do* shut up, Helen,' Gideon admonished, lazily, stretching his legs out in such a way as to display his angelic body in all its glory.

Furiously, Helen rounded on him and both of her personas waded into the melee, with the phrases 'fucking show-off', 'pervert' and a whole lot more f-ing this and f-ing that collapsing into a largely indistinguishable pit of abuse to which Gideon appeared grandly immune. Dennis sighed again, waited until she paused for breath and then in that split second leapt in with, 'As Murray is new here, why don't you tell him a little bit about yourself, Helen?'

'Why should I? He's nothing to do with me and for that matter nor are you. I shouldn't even be here,' she protested, shrilly, although the intervention appeared to have successfully derailed her rant at Gideon and she reverted to almost inaudible muttering, her eyes darting around the group suspiciously.

'All right, Gideon. Why don't *you* start us off, then?'

Unlike Helen, the heavenly body was only too pleased to be given the floor—something of which Dennis was no doubt well aware.

'Hmm. Well, I'm a *naturist* and I can only function when I'm naked. Unfortunately, some ignorant, repressed people don't like this lifestyle and in consequence I've been forced before the Courts for indecency more times than I can count, but it's no good. I can't wear clothes. I just can't. Brrrr!'

He shuddered and Murray was left wondering if this was an expression of his distaste for wearing clothes or alternatively an acknowledgement of the cold, for even in this little room with its gas fire, it was almost glacial. He longed to shoot a glance at Gideon's extremities just to see how inured they really were to the plummeting temperature, but didn't dare and kept his eyes firmly averted.

Gideon's been in a lot of trouble over the years and this has led to discussions in our group about the rights of the individual over the masses. What do *you* think, Murray?'

This wasn't at all what Murray had expected, but Gideon was staring at him intently and he said carefully, 'Well, personally I don't mind at all, but knowing what some people are like, I'm not surprised that he's been in trouble. Perhaps the law should be changed.'

'Groovy,' enthused Gideon, his pectorals rippling in another show of undisguised exhibitionism.

'Changed how?' asked Dennis, evidently intent on pursuing any possible discussion with some semblance of decorum and order.

'Well, perhaps people could get medical exemptions. Something like that.' For a moment Murray tried to imagine Gideon in a series of different jobs turning up for work naked, only to be distracted by the man himself leaping to his feet with a brief display of something resembling tribal dancing.

Murray couldn't bring himself to watch—all that gyrating! Good God!! Had he not witnessed it with his own eyes he would never have imagined that someone like Gideon could have existed, let alone survive to adulthood Dennis seemed similarly appalled, because he positively bawled at him. *'Sit down*, Gideon, before I send you out!'

Then, with an almost seamless de-escalation to normal volume he turned back to Murray and said calmly, 'Thank you, that's very interesting.'

'I'm schizophrenic,' Helen shrieked, suddenly.

'We'd never have guessed.' This comment in the most laconic of tones came from a man dressed in a stripey robe with baggy trousers poking out underneath. He had a red, jolly face and was balding, with a crown of white hair, putting Murray in mind of a debauched version of *Joseph & the Technicolour Dreamcoat*.

Helen rounded on him as if it was her alter ego who'd spoken and began an exhibition akin to two fishwives having a spat, hammer and tongs.

'Any more comments like that and I'll send you out,' Dennis yelled above the din, then he turned back to Murray again and said, 'As Helen's told you, she's schizophrenic...' Leaning towards her he asked slowly and carefully as if to a child, 'Do *you* want to tell your story, Helen, or shall I?'

But she didn't seem to hear him and he continued, 'Well, we don't know very much, but she was abandoned as a new born baby—probably in the early 1950's—and was brought up in an institution where her condition wasn't recognised, so she spent a lot of time in isolation because they didn't know what else to do with her. Then eventually she was released as an adult and since then has yo-yoed between being sectioned and sleeping rough. She has medication but doesn't always take it and that's when the psychosis steps in and she enters this dual personality.'

There was silence when he'd finished speaking except for Helen, who didn't seem to register that she'd been the subject under discussion and continued muttering to herself.

'So what about *you*, Barnabus?' asked Dennis.

'I'm easy. I'm just an alcoholic,' came the airy reply, apparently without regret.

'And....come on, there's a bit more than that,' Dennis prompted, evidently having been through this routine before.

Barnabus sighed, as if appeasing a persistent child. 'My parents ran a pub in Leeds in the 1920s and 30s and from as early as I can remember I was given alcohol to drink. The customers found it funny, I suppose. I also thought it was quite funny—that is until I became an alcoholic at about the age of about 18. I left school with no qualifications but couldn't stick at any job, then I was conscripted into the Army during the War and I did quite well there, surprisingly. Then when the War was over it all went downhill again. I got married but she threw me out after a year or so and then I became a tramp. That was nearly 30 years ago and I've been a tramp ever since.'

Dennis hurried to fill in what he evidently considered to be an important gap in this account. 'Barnabus has a very erratic temper as a result of his alcoholism and even when sober can be very verbally aggressive. He tends to voluntarily strike up conversations with strangers he meets along the way, but then becomes irrationally angry with them for no apparent reason and starts shouting.'

'The temper, the temper…it just comes out of nowhere,' Barnabus confirmed, his expression a tragic mask.

'He feels a lot of resentment towards his parents for their stupidity and ignorance in ruining his life and that's what lies behind the anger issues,' Dennis clarified.

Murray could see why Barnabus was pissed off and he shuddered, wondering what Claude and Josephine would have made of that compete absence of parental accountability. Still, their own record was hardly spotless, given that they'd abandoned Frank in a home and lied to Murray all his life.

There were two other men and two women present, three of whom were quiet and middle aged, while the other was a gangly youth with an insolent expression who was introduced as Oswald. Murray felt sure that he'd seen him stacking shelves in one of the local supermarkets and as if reading his mind the youth fixed him with a disdainful stare and announced through a mouthful of bubble gum that he'd been diagnosed with borderline personality disorder.

He blew out an especially large bubble as if in defiance of Murray's gaze and then swore violently as it exploded over his nose and chin.

Gideon yawned. 'Actually, he's just thick,' he elaborated, at which Oswald leapt at him and a violent scuffle ensued, ending only when Barnabus and Dennis physically intervened to pull Oswald off—unfortunately not before the latter's Doc Marten had made contact with the exposed nether region of his opponent.

Gideon was left flailing and bellowing as Dennis rounded on the offending youth with a prolonged diatribe, the general thrust of which was that he'd be sending a report to his psychiatrist and that he was banned from these meetings forthwith.

'I was provoked!' snarled Oswald, who now seemed oblivious to the bubble gum which still covered much of his face. He glowered unrepentantly at Gideon, who by now was huddled in his chair, his chin tucked into his knees and whimpering quietly.

Dennis seemed slightly out of breath after his outburst, but he gathered himself together sufficiently to say shortly, 'Get your coat on and get out.' Then he turned to Murray and reiterated, 'We don't tolerate any physical violence here. It's the number one rule.'

As Oswald marched unrepentantly out of the room he turned back and addressed Murray directly. 'Can you swim?'

He was obviously intending to be provocative in some way, so Murray simply responded, 'Why?'

To which the youth answered impudently, 'Because if you can't, you'd better fuckin' learn, hadn't you?' and marched out, clutching a dirty sherpa jacket under one arm.

I told you, he's a fucking nutter,' Gideon assured them all, now addressing no one in particular. He seemed to be slightly recovering his equanimity following Oswald's assault and cautiously rolled out his body again to its former, dazzling, state of display.

'You should know better than to provoke him,' Dennis said, sharply and then, to the group in general: 'Oswald has issues interacting with others, as you saw there, but he's held down a job for several months now and we've been trying to build up his confidence.' He took a deep breath and then directed his gaze at Murray again before continuing, 'Well, you've heard a fair bit about us, now, so why don't you tell us something about yourself?'

Murray cleared his throat. They all seemed pretty wacko to him, but they made as good an audience as any and perhaps even better than most as for the next few minutes at least there would be no distractions. He noticed that even the boring-looking ones who hadn't said anything yet seemed suddenly more attentive and were watching him intently.

'My name is Murray,' he announced rather grandly to the silent room and waited a moment for that to sink in, before continuing, 'Of course, it's not my real name, because sadly my real parents—at least one of whom I believe is descended from the aristocracy—gave me up at birth to adoptive parents for political or social reasons, possibly because I was illegitimate.

'Unfortunately, insurmountable hurdles have been put before me all my life in an effort to prevent me from determining my real origins. For example, from an early age hypnosis was employed as just one of the extreme measures which my adoptive parents resorted to in perpetuating the deception...'

Expectantly he looked around his little audience and was satisfied to see that they were completely agog, as well they might be, realising for the first time that the son of a Duke—or even Royalty—was in their midst.

He continued, 'Either fortunately or unfortunately depending on how you want to look at it, I was born with exceptional intellectual abilities—some might say genius—which has earned me a great deal of money, but more about that in a minute.

'It was *my* conceptual and mathematical theories which produced the first computer, *Colossus*, and since then I've written music which put me on an earning par with the most successful composers of the day. However, because these powers emerged during war time, my authorship was kept anonymous because of the general shroud of secrecy which affected all areas of life during those years...'

He looked around the room expectantly and was pleased to note the screaming silence. Satisfied, he announced, 'As a result, the copyrights which should have been mine were never recognised and my authorship has been attributed to anonymous collaborative efforts. However, I continued my musical output post-War and earned vast sums which were ploughed back into reinvestment in other countries without my knowledge. So again, I was sidelined and my attempts to claim back these copyrights have been obstructed at every turn. However, I haven't yet given up, even though I should now be retired and enjoying the fruits of my labours—not to mention the benefits I've brought to this country.

'However, those responsible for my situation—including both my real *and* adoptive families and also the government—wish to keep me in a position of subservience, that is to say on a minimum income and in a council flat, moreover surrounded by invisible spies called goons who keep watch 24 hours a day. I've also been hounded by doppelgangers, and it's only my extreme mental resilience which has enabled me to block out their activities to some degree. However, every time I let my guard down, they come back.

'Obviously this persecution is unlawful, but unfortunately the situation is impossible to prove in a court of law and all I can do is to continue trying to improve my circumstances. I still write more saleable material than almost anyone else and have also produced paintings that the most discriminating market influencers are keen to invest in.

'I'm hoping that the advent of computers in the business world will eventually enable me to trace the copyrights due to me and once that's achieved, I should be able to freely publicise my achievements, including major works hanging in the *National Gallery* and others regularly sold by *Christies* and *Sothebys*. And furthermore, I've written or revised music for the annual *Proms* and the world's opera houses, not to mention supergroups such as the *Beatles*, *Queen* and *Abba*.

'As I speak, my work is fuelling colossal pay and bonuses for the favoured few, while I languish unacclaimed and unrecognised. The nature of British politics appears to be to suppress any information deemed subversive and this brings me back to my birthright, because there are powerful people who wish to keep my existence a secret and for that reason I'm not permitted to rise to any degree of wealth, fame or glory.'

He finished with a flourish of his arm and noted with satisfaction the resounding hush in the room, finally broken by Dennis who seemed more lost for words than usual but managed a loaded, '*Well...*' which was promptly interrupted by Gideon lowering the tone with, 'I've never heard such a load of bloody balderdash in my entire life!'

Murray regarded him coldly. 'Well, I wouldn't expect anything else from you. That's the very attitude by which the powers-that-be have sought to subdue me for my entire life.'

Helen giggled and then shouted at her alter ego and fell back to muttering quietly.

'I realise that this is all quite a lot to take on board, but don't worry. As I said, I've been forced into the most impecunious circumstances and although you now know at least some of the truth, I don't expect any preferential treatment.' Murray adopted what he hoped was an affable expression.

'Thank you, Murray, and Gideon, please apologise or I'll be writing to your Probation Officer,' threatened Dennis.

Gideon scowled.

'There's no need. His reaction is quite normal and it's for that reason that I very rarely talk about myself,' Murray offered, in a conciliatory tone.

'Well, you're certainly making up for it now,' intervened Gideon, rudely.

'Shut up!' roared Dennis and then after making another visible effort to control himself he turned back to Murray. 'Gideon has no business being so rude and I apologise on his behalf. We operate a policy of total respect here,' he finished, turning back to glare at the fallen angel.

'Oh, all right. *Soz* old man,' Gideon volunteered, raising his eyebrows to heaven.

'Can I ask a question?' asked Barnabus, suddenly, helpfully distracting from what had become a rather intense three-way exchange.

'If it's polite,' warned Dennis.

Barnabus turned to Murray. 'What's all this about you being subversive? Why do they think that?' he asked.

'It's just that certain people who are high up, either in politics or socially or both, have an interest in keeping my existence from public knowledge, that's all I meant,' explained Murray.

'But why?'

'Possibly because I was illegitimate and there's still a lot of stigma around that sort of thing in those circles, but I can't say for sure because my investigations have been blocked at every turn. However, *past sins cast long shadows* as they say and I'm fairly sure that it's all to do with protecting someone else's reputation at the cost of my own well-being,' Murray explained.

Barnabus looked as if he wanted to ask something else, but Dennis shut him down with a look and then said to Murray, 'Usually we talk about what we've done since the last meeting and share information about jobs, soup kitchens, how to get round the bureaucracy of collecting dole…all that sort of thing. Most of us are on a combination of benefits, medications, suspended sentences, on probation…' He looked around. 'Has anyone got anything to say, while we still have a few minutes left?'

But everyone seemed suddenly and inexplicably sapped of the will to live, so the little group wound up early, with Dennis making a note on his clip board that the other supposed new arrivals had never actually arrived.

Murray felt quite sombre as he walked the couple of miles home, threading his way through a series of well-worn short cuts. They were all as nutty as fruit cakes and even Dennis had seemed a few pence short of the full quid, but he'd quite enjoyed it nevertheless and had even surprised himself with the eloquence of his expression. It hadn't been easy to give such a succinct, yet comprehensive account and given that he'd had no preparation to speak of, it had all gone rather well.

Moreover, there was no doubt that he'd been easily the sanest person in the room and even if he took nothing else away from the meeting, that, at least, was worth hanging on to.

Chapter 10

January 1976
Leastways, SW3
Murray's move to the council flat at *Leastways* had gone relatively smoothly and the furniture which had been positively sparse in *Du Kane Court* had filled it quite nicely.

Once he'd got used to the idea, he didn't even mind reverting back to renting rather than home ownership as it gave him much more flexibility to move quickly if he needed to and in the meantime he had a comforting wad of cash in the bank. Besides, it was only the British who had this obsession with home ownership as nearly everyone else in the world was more than happy to rent.

Inevitably he'd noticed a slight lowering of the tone regarding the area and his neighbours, but on the plus side they were quiet and didn't bother him. It was all a far cry from what he'd been born to, but what was the saying? *Them's the breaks*?

He was still basking in the reflected glory of his speech to the *Group Therapy* bunch and was particularly impressed with himself for remembering so many different elements of his campaign—not least those copyright payments. It wasn't that he'd ever *forgotten* about them, but they'd certainly got pushed to the back of his mind while so much else was going on. No doubt that was what the powers-that-be intended, but his ad-hoc performance had been yet another example of how his intellect always shone through.

It got him to wondering if he might be able to use the Library to research copyright and potentially explore the chances of pursuing his claim in the law courts. He must be owed hundreds of thousands of pounds and he was damned if he'd give it up without a fight.

A few days after the meeting he had an unprecedented letter from Claude to let him know that he and Josephine had just moved to a village called Fivehead, where he'd bought a smallholding of 30 acres and was going to keep Jersey cows, selling the milk locally and eventually making his own butter, if all went well. He gave a new address and telephone number and said that Murray would be welcome to visit—an offer that was far-fetched to say the least, given that there had been no contact between them for almost two years now, and that occasion hadn't exactly ended well—especially for the smashed teacup.

It wasn't in Murray's nature to be destructive or violent, but he really had been pushed to the limit that day—and throughout his whole life, for that matter.

He reckoned that the smallholding must have cost a fair bit—more than they'd get for the little thatched cottage at any rate—and he speculated as to whether his father's rich cousin, *Old Barn*, had helped out, using up cash that was meant to be for *Murray's* inheritance. It really was sickening.

He wasn't working until 4 pm and on impulse decided to use his spare time that day to go to the Library. He'd feel calmer there and besides, he really had to start researching those copyrights. In fact, it was unforgiveable that he'd left it so long and thank God the group therapy had brought it all back into razor sharp focus once more. He was even rather looking forward to their next session.

* * * * * * *

Dobbler's Den, Fivehead, Somerset

Claude leant heavily on the wooden, 5-bar gate and looked out at his 25 Jersey cows, grazing serenely on the 15-acre field. They'd soon get through what little grass was available at this time of year and he'd have to rotate them between the two fields, probably supplementing with cow nuts until the lush grass returned in two or three months' time.

Setting up had been expensive and time consuming, but he'd had plenty of time to plan for it because the venture had been a long time coming. Unfortunately, he'd been forced to wait until he was 69 years old because he'd needed Josephine's financial input and being younger than him, she'd only just qualified for her full pension. All the same, she was fully supportive and had even helped him with all the research.

His bible for the last 18 months had been the *Herd Book*, first produced in 1880 and full of quaint and instructive advice, especially with regard to breeding. With due deference to tradition, much lineage was given over to the pioneers of Jersey herds in England as well as to more recent successes and as a result Claude had travelled far and wide in his bid to build up the perfect herd.

As a result he could truthfully say that he'd established a relationship with each of his animals and certainly knew all the cows by name. They were a friendly and affectionate bunch and in even this short time he'd become extremely attached to them, although he had his favourites, specifically Buttercup and her male calf which he'd named Pug, on account of his wide-eyed expression.

Two other favourites were a particularly beautiful cow called Brunette and a very productive one called Violet. In fact, they were all beautiful, with their graceful carriage, tan muzzles, black pointing and thick coats in a variety of tints from light reddish brown to duns and fawns. He could have stood and stared at them all day and would have done, had there been sufficient hours available to him.

Places like this didn't come up very often, but luckily he'd heard about it on the grapevine and the transaction had been done very amicably with a little help from *Old Barn*, for which he was eternally grateful. She'd get her money back, but it would take a few years to set things up properly.

He'd been sorely tempted not to write that conciliatory letter to Murray because he honestly felt that—sad to say—he could quite happily never have seen or heard anything of him again. This made him feel guilty because for better or worse Murray *was* his son, but for as long as he could remember, their intermittent contact had only ever been confrontational, so what was he supposed to feel? It would hardly have been realistic if Claude had welcomed him with open arms, only to be repaid with more abuse and corresponding collateral damage.

He wished that it was possible to put that whole, ghastly chapter of his life behind him for ever and with Grace long dead, Murray claiming to be somebody else, Frank in an institution and Miriam thousands of miles away from everything in Australia, it should have been easy enough to do, but somehow real life didn't work like that. In the end it had been Josephine who'd insisted that for his own peace of mind he had to do the right thing and leave the door open, so that was what he'd done. Besides, there was very little chance that anything would come of it.

The early part of Claude's life now seemed quite surreal—or at least, the part after he'd met Grace. She'd been so beautiful and talented that it was hardly surprising he'd fallen in love with her, not to mention that his best friend Roland had been engaged to her sister. It had all seemed meant to be: two talented officers in the *Royal Artillery* marrying two beautiful sisters, but things which seemed too good to be true usually *were* too good to be true and this had been no exception.

The marriage had taken a hit early on because they were so different and there'd been rows. She was extrovert and loved parties, while he was quiet and shy and in what little free time was available to him, the last thing he'd wanted to do was go dashing off out to some frivolous 'do' where he didn't even know anyone.

He'd hoped that motherhood might change her—or at least bring them closer together—but then when Frank had arrived and turned out to be a Mongol...well, everything had been ten times worse and it had seemed like the end of the world. As if a curse was hanging over them. He blamed himself, because being the elder of the two, he should have heeded the warning signs regarding their incompatible dispositions and never got married. Even his mother had warned him that she was on the rebound from another relationship, but of course he hadn't listened.

Grace had gone into a serious depression after the birth. Not much was known about Mongol babies at that time, but he wasn't expected to live very long—only about 12 years at the most the doctors had said. They'd both tried to love him, but it had been difficult, given how handicapped he was.

Then Miriam had been born and things looked up a bit, but by that time war was looming and there hadn't been much time to enjoy normal parenthood before he'd been posted to Singapore with the family in tow. They'd left Frank with his grandmother—it had seemed the best thing to do all round—and once they were abroad Grace had come out of herself again. Quite how much of that had been to do with being free of a handicapped child was difficult to say, because they'd also walked straight into a very lively ex-pat social scene and Claude hadn't dared analyse things too deeply. At the end of the day it had simply been enough that she'd become more like her old self again.

Murray had been born two years later in Singapore and he'd been a normal, alert child, although only 18 months old at the point that the family had been forced to flee to Australia, just before the Japanese invasion. Claude had naturally stayed at his Army post and accordingly been herded into *Changi Jail* along with everybody else who'd been left behind. Thanks to the oriental obsession with status, officers had been treated very marginally better than the ranks, but even so, it had been bad enough.

Dysentery and scabies had been common killers, but just as many had died from starvation and the tortuous punishments devised by twisted and brutal minds.

When he'd finally heard that Grace had died—months after the event—he'd felt a curious mixture of sensations. Grief because she'd been so young and beautiful and was the mother of his children, but guilty relief that at least this way they'd be spared the trauma of almost inevitable divorce. It was clear even then that if he survived *Changi* he'd be even more introspective and retiring than before and it would have driven her up the wall. Moreover, knowing that she was dead had given him an even greater incentive to live, given that otherwise his children would have been orphans.

When the schizophrenia had first emerged in Murray he'd been about 16 or 17 and Claude had put it down to eccentricity, but as a GP Josephine had recognised the signs immediately and managed to get him assessed and on medication very quickly. Everything had seemed all right until that fateful helicopter crash had brought it back with a vengeance, because until then he'd had an extremely successful career: *Sandhurst*, the *11th Hussars*... He must have been all right up to that point, because the Army was notoriously particular about everything to do with physical *and* mental health.

Claude had a feeling that one of the reasons Miriam had chosen not to marry or have children was because she didn't want to perpetuate the gene on Grace's side of the family which had caused depression and related problems in several of the boys, going back two or three generations. He wished that she hadn't settled in Australia because being separated from her long-term had been painful for him, but the most important thing was that she seemed happy and he'd learned not to hope for more.

He sighed. Grace. Frank. Miriam. Murray... The only part of his early life which hadn't ended in tragedy was Miriam, although she hadn't escaped unscathed either and they hadn't seen each other for 15 years now. It was even possible that he wouldn't *ever* see her again, as although they corresponded regularly, she showed no inclination to visit the Motherland, and he couldn't really blame her—there was too much water under the bridge.

Josephine was his strength now as he hadn't had much of his own for a long time—certainly since Murray's accident six years ago. However, since moving to Fivehead he'd felt a renewed zest for life which had taken him by surprise. Was it possible that the wheel of fortune had creaked around again and that a herd of Jersey cows had generated its own magic?

The calf he'd named Pug frolicked around his mother in a rare moment of winter sunshine and his spirits rose. As he turned away and walked towards the house it crossed his mind how astounding it was that a single life could undergo such an immense see-saw of experiences—the comforts of an upper-middle class life, the horrors of *Changi Jail*, the chaos of a cursed marriage made in the idealism of youth and finally the tranquillity of a successful marriage made in the wisdom of middle age.

He could only hope and pray that the fickle wheel of fortune would go easy on him in his remaining years.

Chelsea Library, Old Town Hall, Kings Road

Murray was hugely excited. It was two weeks since his first visit to the Library, since which time he'd spent *hours* in the legal section researching copyright law and had come across some very interesting names.

It was when he'd been reading about various legal cases which had taken place over the last 30 years that he'd come across a fascinating claim in 1972 relating to a Charles Alers Hankey—at that time Viscount Winchester—who'd taken a company called *Rollout Records* to court over a £10,000 claim for breach of copyright concerning a number of songs written for various artists. Whether he'd written the songs himself or had been patron to the songwriter wasn't clear, but it wasn't the facts of the case that resonated with Murray so much as the name of Alers Hankey. It struck him like a lightning bolt and he knew straight away that this was a name from his past—possibly one that had first come up in those hypnosis sessions.

What a stroke of luck that instead of eradicating the name from his memory for ever as intended, a reverse effect had now been kick-started.

It immediately occurred to him that this was the connection he'd been seeking and yet he'd come across it by pure chance while searching for something else. It was all a bit hard to take in, but he immediately requested a copy of *Burke's Peerage* to be sent from another Library and spent five days on tenterhooks waiting for it to arrive.

When it finally did, he pored over it for hours, drinking in the family details and noting with delight that Charles was now the 7th Duke of Hampshire and lived in an 18th century castle near Portsmouth, having succeeded his father two years earlier.

Murray calculated that he himself was almost certainly the eldest, illegitimate son of the 6th Duke—so the half-brother of Charles—and wondered if his real mother might possibly have been Grace? Certainly, she would have been sufficiently attractive and vivacious to attract men from any walk of life.

He did more research on the 6th Duke and to his amazement discovered that he'd served in the 3rd Battalion of the Coldstream Guards and had been in the Middle East during WW2. Singapore wasn't technically in the Middle East, but nevertheless it put the Duke and Grace in roughly the same area at the same time during the War.

It was truly elucidating to be suddenly in possession of so much knowledge and moreover the knowledge that he'd longed for all his life. It was as if a weight had been lifted from his shoulders and he assiduously investigated the wealth and connections of his new-found family. Charles had a younger brother and sister, although the sister had died in childbirth some years back, which just went to show how right Murray had been to dismiss Miriam as an imposter.

So his *real* sister was sadly dead and he'd never even known her, but come to that, would he ever know any of them? Should he even try?

He decided in the meantime to gather together as much evidence as possible in order to prove beyond reasonable doubt that he *was* the illegitimate son of the 6th Duke.

Over the next few weeks he researched the family back as far as he could and discovered a direct line back to George Duke of Clarence, brother to the last *Plantagenet* Kings Edward IV and Richard III in the 15th century. He was almost beside himself with joy and drew up a detailed family tree right up to the 6th Duke and himself.

The family also had a French branch and from what he could gather they still owned land in Bordeaux. It was all rather complicated and sometimes he felt a little overwhelmed, but determination and the conviction that he was on the right track drove him on.

The Alers Hankey Coat of Arms had been granted to the 2nd Duke in 1815 for services rendered at the *Battle of Waterloo* and was another huge excitement. The image was of two golden lions standing on their hind legs and facing each other against a royal blue background with the words *Fortis et Fidelis*—strong and brave. Nevertheless, despite the thrills all this elicited, he was quite relieved to move on from heraldry, because it was so dense as to be almost impenetrable.

Murray's problem—or at least, one of them—was that his principal proof of being the 6th Duke's son was something *he* knew to be irrevocably true as a result of the throwback to hypnosis which he'd undergone as a child, yet it would be impossible to prove it to anyone else and for that reason he reluctantly decided not to contact the family, because any attempt to gain formal recognition wouldn't stand up to scrutiny and would almost certainly also cause bad feeling.

To his surprise this decision didn't affect him as badly as he'd thought it might, because the most important thing was that he'd discovered his roots and that alone had catapulted him out of the abyss into which anonymity had flung him all those years ago. Moreover, it would now be his for ever and nobody could ever take it away.

He bought an A4-sized art book and began to meticulously record all that he'd discovered, detailing the genealogy, heraldry and history of all the Dukes going back to 1815 and then slightly less detailed links beyond that, back to the Plantagenets. However, throughout all this he made a point of taking days off to visit Frank and despite his complete immersion in the Alers Hankey project it was no hardship, because without the occasional break he couldn't possibly have sustained the intensity required.

His days away were an almost 100% transition from what felt like extreme academia to a world of the utmost simplicity and the combination brought him enormous satisfaction. In fact, he felt happier than he'd ever been.

He tried to tell Frank a little bit about it in the simple terms of a fairy story: he'd discovered that his real family was very rich and lived in a castle. That, at least, got Frank's attention, so he promised him that quite soon they'd drive down and see it, given that it was only about 50 miles from Hove. Murray promised that they'd go when he finished the book he was compiling with all its beautiful family trees. He'd even meticulously copied and painted the coat of arms and thanked God that he was sufficiently multi-talented not to need to involve anyone else in the project.

But perhaps the most exciting stage of his being catapulted into the aristocracy was what he'd do last—change his name by deed poll and claim his role in the Alers Hankey story once and for all.

* * * * * * *

April 1976, London

It was imperative that Murray's adoptive family—or fake family as he now preferred to call them—should know that he'd discovered the truth, but he wanted to wait until all the loose ends had been tied up before that happened. In other words, he had to finish the book, visit the castle—at least from the outside—and change his name.

The subject of the name change caused him some indecision. Alers Hankey was straightforward enough, but what for the Christian names? The 6th Duke had been called Hedley and his first legitimate son was Charles, but going back through the family tree, the names which occurred most frequently were Arthur and Ernest, so he decided on those two. Arthur Ernest Alers Hankey had a very nice ring to it and he immediately felt extremely comfortable with it.

The problem remained that he had absolutely no idea of how to go about the whole *Deed Poll* business, but on recourse to his friends at the *Citizen's*

Advice Bureau, discovered that a £12 cheque and a letter to the *Royal Courts of Justice* should be sufficient to start the ball rolling. He was advised that it would take several weeks, but as he was still finishing the book and had yet to visit the castle, that hardly mattered. It was just a matter of time and then they'd all know. Everyone would know, soon enough.

Chapter 11

May 1976
London/Hampshire

By the first week of May Murray was ready—or at least, Arthur Ernest Alers Hankey was ready—to let everyone know who he really was. The compilation of his family history was complete and his name had been changed, although getting people to use it was quite another matter. His workplace had been most reluctant to change their records and he'd had to insist in the most uncompromising terms before the girl in accounts had sulkily backed down. It had been a similar story with his bank and even Frank was flatly refusing to conform.

'I like Murray, I don't like Arthur,' he insisted, stubbornly.

'Well then, call me Ernest, that's my second name.'

'I don't like Ernest either.' And he refused to be persuaded.

Murray thought that he could probably have gone through all the names in the alphabet and all of them would have been turned down, so having conceded defeat as gracefully as possible he was more than a little put out when Frank said suddenly, 'I like *Claude*.'

'But that's your father's name.'

'I know.'

'Has he been to see you?'

'No.'

Frank could be annoying like that and conversations about anything remotely important frequently couldn't be followed through to any logical conclusion. Murray was most anxious to know why—if Claude hadn't been to see him for a long time—Frank even remembered his name, but there was no point trying to open a conversation along those lines because he'd just shut down.

However, as he was now accustomed to making allowances for Frank that he wouldn't have dreamed of making for anybody else, he didn't let it ruin his new-found euphoria.

The one remaining task yet to be completed was their visit to *Alers Castle* in Hampshire. Having originally imagined it to be on the outskirts of Portsmouth, Murray discovered on further investigation that it was actually 12 miles north of there, somewhere outside the tiny village of Hambledon.

Because the castle was in the middle of nowhere, Murray took the precaution of ordering an AA route map as the prospect of driving lost around the countryside with Frank map reading wasn't one which he was prepared to countenance. He'd never used one of those maps before, but the lady he'd spoken to on the phone had sworn that it would lead him directly to the castle gates. It was, in fact, the first call he'd made after moving into his new flat and the luxury of having a line again after being cut off for so long was infinitely gratifying.

He studied the map the night before with the intention of committing as much of it to memory as possible and was reassured that it was very direct—due west from Hove for most of the way and then north-west after reaching a small town called Havant. They didn't even have to touch Portsmouth at all and it should be a very pleasant journey on A-roads all the way and then a small B-road just for the last few miles from Havant.

'You know that today we're going to see the castle that should rightfully be mine?' Murray asked conversationally as they set off.

'No,' replied Frank, blissfully unaware that his disinterest might in any way be irritating.

'Well, we *are*,' said Murray, patiently, and then explained for the umpteenth time. 'It went to someone else because when I was born, my father wasn't married to my mother.'

'Oooh.'

Frank had no idea about marriage, but Murray felt that he'd taken enough on board for now. It did make him a little sad that he didn't have anyone with whom to share the intricate details of his good fortune, as it would have been cathartic to spill it all out to someone who was genuinely interested.

However, Murray didn't really have friends. Just people at work who he got on with all right on that basis, but nobody who he actually met socially for the purpose of talking to them—which was how the process of friendship appeared to operate. What he had with Frank would never be normal, but then if it had been, it probably wouldn't have worked.

He hadn't even shared it with his therapy group yet, because they hadn't met for six weeks on account of Dennis being ill and the next meeting was scheduled for later this week. After that there would be just one more session and then the course would be over. In a way it was fortunate for Murray that there'd been a gap, because he might otherwise have been tempted to spill the beans too soon. It was much better to have got everything proven and recorded for posterity before trying to share it with them.

He'd take the book, of course, and could hardly wait to see the look on Gideon's face when he was definitively proved wrong. Some people were just so cynical that sometimes it seemed as if all integrity and honesty had gone out of the world.

Hambledon was a small, picturesque village whose main claim to fame appeared to be a lengthy association with cricket and they stopped at the roadside next to a large green space called *Broad Halfpenny* which turned out to be a cricket pitch furnished with a quite large wooden pavilion of which the crowning glory was a rather grand clocktower.

Walking a little further down what appeared to be a farm lane, they came to the *Bat & Ball Inn*, currently closed because it was only 10.30 am. Murray considered calling in on the way back, but wasn't sure how it would go down if he took Frank. He'd noticed that people often stared at them in the street and on the beach, but somehow it didn't seem to matter so much when they were outside. Indoors, the unwelcome attention somehow became more focussed and awkward, not to mention that there was less chance of escape.

All around there were fields and woods and it was really very lovely. And to think that all this could have been—if not actually *his*—at least on his doorstep. For the first time since being punctured by the Alers Hankey dart, Murray felt a lump in his throat: like a rejected child, or a young man disinherited, or someone unwanted and unloved. Even unknown. It was strange to simultaneously belong and yet *not* to belong.

A tear rolled down his cheek and to his surprise Frank said, 'It's all right Murray, the car's not far away.'

He had to smile, because to Frank everything was so simple and the sort of things you cried about were when you were tired or—worse—hungry.

He said nothing to set Frank straight and thanked God that his dear brother would always bring him down to earth. That was why some people said they had animals and it was very true. No disrespect to Frank intended, but an uncomplicated being—either two or four legged—could put things into perspective and that could make all the difference between coping and not coping.

Once they'd returned to the car, Murray consulted the *AA* map again. They were only a couple of miles away now and apart from farmland there wasn't anything else marked on the route until they arrived, at which point the castle should be on the right. He checked the mileage and they set off, his heart beating like a child's on *Christmas Eve*. In contrast, Frank gazed unconcernedly out of the window humming something unintelligible and Murray rather envied him.

They came to a long section of stone wall about four foot high, which Murray guessed marked the boundary of the castle and he parked on the grass verge, so that he and Frank could walk alongside it and possibly get a better view. There was parkland on the other side of the wall and mature trees, but a tall house was visible, set well back from the road—some 200 yards or so Murray estimated— and its beauty almost took his breath away.

It was a delightfully asymmetrical building comprising five different sections of three or four storeys, all of them neatly castellated at roof level except for the furthermost, right-hand side where a small, pitched roof presided over a burgeoning wisteria which had unfurled over the greater part of the brickwork below.

Next to it was a taller, very narrow tower with a weather vane on top but no windows and then the main section—again of three storeys—where a fine, castellated porch and an abundance of Gothic windows spoke of beauty and light within. To the left of that was a taller, narrower tower which gloried in a single set of miscellaneous windows on each of its four levels and then finally on the far left was a wider tower, devoid of any windows except for a tiny set of three arches at the very top, this furthermost part of the castle being partly hidden by tall, white willows whose graceful upper branches gently swept the battlements with long, luxurious fronds.

A gravel drive swept along the front of the house and a lovely lawn graced by mature trees formed a velvety bridge leading onto the parkland and then to the road.

To the right of the house was a high stone wall which stretched the length of the lawn and was resplendent with its own tall, Gothic archway and adjoining tower. It may have led to a rear garden, stables or even a kitchen garden...there was no telling. Murray thought that it was the most beautiful building that he'd ever seen and he drank in the sight of it, temporarily lost for words.

Frank sat down on the verge and started playing with the *Triumph Spitfire* car that he'd brought with him.

Desiring to record this wonder for both posterity and the Alers Hankey scrapbook, Murray took his camera out of its case and screwed on the wide-angle lens before leaning as far as he could over the top of the wall. He took a couple of shots but felt that the picture would be a lot clearer with a 50 mm lens and that meant getting a bit nearer. He would have liked to tell Frank to stay where he was for 15 minutes while he trespassed alone, but didn't dare leave him so there was nothing else for it—Frank would simply have to come along for the ride.

'Come on, Frank,' he ordered, impulsively.

'Where are we going?'

'A bit closer to the house. We'll get some better photographs that way.'

'All right.'

It was convenient that Frank had no concept whatsoever of trespass or even of anything at all to do with breaking rules, let alone laws.

About 50 yards further on they came to the driveway entrance and using the shelter of a wooded area between the parkland and the road they edged considerably closer to the house, with Murray periodically reeling Frank back behind cover as he wandered erratically, oblivious of need for subterfuge.

The limited information which Murray had been able to get hold of prior to his visit had said that there had been a house on this site since medieval times, but that this one was early 18th century and it certainly had all the refinement and elegance of the classic Georgian houses, but also that wonderful, Gothic influence with its arches and castellated sections.

He felt proud, sad and wistful all at once. If only he could have knocked on the door, explained who he was and been welcomed as part of the family—although come to that, there wasn't anyone, anywhere in the country who would have welcomed him in any capacity except for Frank at *Marlow Place* in Hove. It didn't seem much to ask of his kith and kin, but even amid the rosy glow of his imaginings, Murray wasn't tempted to try it because morally and ethically the castle should be his and it was therefore inevitable that the current occupants would regard him as a threat.

And to tell the truth, he couldn't say hand on heart that given half a chance, he *wouldn't* want a piece of it. Who wouldn't?

He could have stayed there for hours, but Frank was getting restless and he was just about to suggest that they head back to the car when a harsh voice behind them made him nearly jump out of his skin.

'What the *hell* do you think you're doing here?!' and then without waiting for a reply. 'You're trespassing. I'll have the law on you. Bloody *Press*—you just can't keep away, can you?!'

Frank was affected by the shock of this rude interruption even more than

Murray had been and with a shriek of alarm began galloping off back the way they'd come, even before the man had finished speaking, his ungainly gait weaving erratically from side to side.

Murray exploded in anger. 'Now look what you've done you raving imbecile!' he shouted, and momentarily fought the impulse to punch the man on the nose before a modicum of restraint prevailed and he raced off after Frank instead, eventually bringing him down with something approaching a rugby tackle on soft ground about 50 yards away.

Fortunately Frank appeared to be unhurt by this abrupt end to his flight, but was still crying and shaking when the man, slightly abashed, approached for the second time and at a rather more leisurely pace. 'You get out right now!' he ordered, although slightly less sure of himself now.

'It's *his* house, you raving imbecile,' sobbed Frank, in an opportune display of the mimicry which was one of his charms.

'I *am* a member of the family,' Murray clarified, equally as severe as the man himself had been, 'And now if you don't mind, *you'd* better clear off. You've already done enough damage and we are, in any case, going now.'

It was the first time that Murray had got a proper look at the man since their inopportune introduction and his impression wasn't favourable. He was probably a gamekeeper from the way he was dressed in mud-spattered tweeds and cap, not to mention the shotgun he was carrying. He looked an unsavoury type with bushy sideburns, cheeks whipped up by the wind or booze or both and narrow, cunning eyes which now darted between Murray and Frank.

'Raving imbecile,' Frank repeated, idly, his words now directed to the barrel of the shotgun which was pointing in their general direction.

The gamekeeper looked nonplussed and might have said a good deal more had Murray given him the opportunity, but luckily they were already close to the entrance and had disappeared from view behind the stone wall before he'd recovered his wits.

'Bloody meglomaniac! *No* bloody manners. I've got a good mind to write and complain about him,' Murray muttered, as offended as if he had, indeed, been *King of the Castle*.

Frank had already forgotten about the fright he'd had—it was sometimes a relief and sometimes annoying, but he really *did* live in the moment, which was why it was so curious to Murray that he would remember something as oblique and distant as his father's Christian name.

On impulse he asked, 'Do you know your surname, Frank?'

'Frank.'

'No, your other name.'

'No.'

'Does Woodall mean anything to you?'

'Yes, that's my name.'

Murray sighed. 'OK, well in future remember that it's your *surname*, Frank. It used to be my surname too, until I discovered who my *real* family were.'

'I'm your real family.'

Murray didn't want to embark upon the unhelpful process of contradicting him. After all, Frank was effectively the person closest to him in the world, so what did it matter if he was blood or not?

He would have liked to celebrate this introduction to his birthright with a drink at the *Bat & Ball* pub which they'd passed on the way, but was still nervous at the prospect of becoming a focus of attention with Frank in tow. No, he'd have to give the drink a miss this time and besides, the verbal attack they'd just experienced had upset his equilibrium and he didn't feel up to meeting anyone—not even strangers.

His unease receded slightly during the return journey and although he felt emotionally drained, it was mostly in a good way. Ignorant ground staff might come and go, but the Castle and his family name was more than he could ever have dreamed and his inheritance would stand for ever.

That night he wrote three letters respectively, to Claude & Josephine, Marjorie & Roland and—after mulling it over for a few minutes—to Miriam. He thought about including his cousins Evie and Tristan, but really there was no point. They'd never been involved and besides, he was quite certain that the news would filter through from the *oldies* before he could say, *Jiminy Cricket*. In fact, he wouldn't have been surprised if the whole letter wasn't painstakingly copied and sent to all and sundry and he was more than happy for that to happen.

He hoped that one or other of the recipients of his letters would be magnanimous enough to accept defeat and congratulate him. If not, it would be a very poor show, although hardly surprising given their record.

He'd had some good quality, pale blue notepaper printed in dark blue with the Alers Hankey coat of arms and his own address alongside. He would have dearly loved to print the castle's real address, but it would just be too impractical and besides, 15, *Leastways*, Chelsea S.W.3 sounded sufficiently impressive—no-one would ever guess that it was a council flat.

Hardest of all had been the decision of whether to give himself a title, so in the end he'd settled for The Hon. Arthur Ernest Alers Hankey Esq., ad Duke of Hampshire. That little 'ad' he felt was inspired, as in Latin it meant 'related to' and satisfactorily conveyed the facts, while simultaneously suggesting to those who didn't read it too carefully that he *was* actually the Duke. Hopefully people might even assume that this was just his *pied a terre* London address and if they did, so much the better. With a smile, he picked up his new fountain pen and started to write.

* * * * * * *

May 15th, 1976
Dobbler's Den, Fivehead, Somerset
It was Marjorie's first visit to *Dobbler's Den* since Claude and Josephine's move a few months earlier, although no one was under the illusion that she'd driven all the way from Sheringham in Norfolk *only* for the purpose of admiring the view. They hadn't spoken about it on the phone but there was no point in any further hedging around what was indisputably the main news of the day, so the moment that Josephine had placed coffee and digestive biscuits in front of her, Marjorie squarely faced the *elephant in the room.*

'You'll have heard from the Duke, then?'

Claude shook his head in disbelief and Josephine spluttered slightly. 'Yes, a couple of days ago. I imagine we all received the same letter.'

Marjorie fished hers out of her handbag and Claude briefly scanned Murray's neat writing. 'Yes, it's the same.'

'I've never known him use ink before, have you?' Marjorie asked.

'I suppose he now has an image to preserve, but really, did he *have* to claim a Dukedom?' Josephine observed dryly.

'Perhaps we should be grateful that he's not claiming the Crown,' Claude quipped, and the women dissolved into giggles.

'Actually, putting that Latin *ad* was a smart move, because it gives exactly the impression that he wants to give, namely that he *is* the Duke,' Josephine mused.

'The thing is...' mused Marjorie, 'it's all harmless enough if it makes him happy and stops these rabid visits denouncing us all for God knows what, but perhaps we ought to decide on some common ground regarding our response. For instance, shall we start calling him Arthur now? And do we even write back? And if we do, what do we say?'

'We need to start calling him Arthur or it will just antagonise him,' said Josephine, adding after a moment, 'But we can stop short of using the title, I think!'

'So, what do we say to his accusation about deceiving him all these years and conspiring to keep him in penury?' Marjorie dipped a digestive into her coffee and regarded them expectantly, oblivious to the tragedy of the dipped portion falling back into her cup and sinking without trace.

Claude took the floor. 'Well, obviously Josephine and I have talked about this over the last couple of days and we decided not to reply immediately—maybe in a few days—and that we'd use his name *minus* the title and say that we're very happy for him and he'll always be welcome here, but not to comment on any of that drivel about us blocking his prospects. I also think that we should at all costs avoid seeing this book of proof which he says he's compiled, because he'll force us to either admit or deny its authenticity and no good could possibly come of it.'

Marjorie nodded. 'All right, well Roland and I will fall into line with that. The last thing we want from him is any more angst, as if I didn't have enough of that at home already.'

Claude and Josephine looked at her in surprise and she explained, 'Yes, it wasn't only about Murray that I needed to talk to you today, because we're having the most frightful time with Tristan.'

There was a pregnant pause until she continued tearfully, 'As you know, he's terribly talented and a couple of years ago put all his money into setting up a business making bespoke wooden toys, but because we've had this terrible slump, the last thing people are buying is luxury toys...'

That much was common knowledge, so her audience sat expectantly as she continued, 'We thought his depression was getting better, but then he started seeing a Harley Street specialist who charged the earth and most worrying of all, let himself simply be *led* by what Triss wanted, so that when Triss said he thought he'd be better off without any medication at all, the man simply agreed and took him off it, just like that!'

She paused and sighed heavily before continuing. Well, naturally that caused the most dreadful insomnia immediately, because everybody knows—I mean, even *non-medical* people know—that long term medication has to be wound down gradually. It really was unforgivably negligent!'

'You ought to report him to the *General Medical Council*,' Claude interrupted her, frowning.

'I think we probably will, but that's not the end of it,' Marjorie continued, wearily. 'We then sent him back to his own doctor, but *he* was away on holiday and the Locum in his place put him on such a high dose of God knows what that he really went quite peculiar. And what with the hay fever and asthma which he already has periodically—it brought all that on and we've just been at our wits' end!'

Her voice broke slightly and Josephine handed her a tissue. 'I'm sorry Marj. Depression is always horribly tricky to treat—what with getting the right drug *and* the right dose, but it does sound as if he's been the victim of terrible incompetence.'

But Marjorie hadn't finished yet. 'And quite apart from all *that*, it looks as if Kathleen's finally had enough and is going to divorce him. I can't blame her because she's tried terribly hard and kept them afloat for some time with *her* wage, but this has been going on for two years now and rather than improving, it's been worse than ever because of all that I've just been telling you about.

'So last month she took the children back to her parents' home in Southsea and Triss is so obsessed with trying to make the business work that he barely even seems to notice they've gone. He's even been building a studio single handed because he hasn't got the money to pay anyone else and is doing all the heavy labouring of bricklaying and cement...*everything*! And yet he can't even pay the mortgage! Roland and I are absolutely out of our depth with it all, it's *such* a mess.'

'It rather puts Murray claiming the Dukedom into perspective,' said Claude and Marjorie smiled, in spite of herself. 'We're trying to work out ways of helping him and have managed to sell a few of his rocking horses to friends of friends at £50 or £70 each, but he doesn't really make very much on them, because the materials are so expensive.'

'We might be able to sell a few round here if you let us have a photograph,' suggested Josephine.

'That's sweet of you dear and I will, but we really need to find a long-term way of paying his mortgage while he builds up the business into some sort of solvency. He's absolutely convinced that it *could* work and is also distraught that he's causing everybody so much concern, although we've tried to hide the worst of it from him.'

'I'm very sorry about it all, Marjorie, but was there anything *specific* that you wanted us to do?' asked Claude.

Marjorie bit her lip. 'This is the hard bit, because I absolutely *hate* to ask, but the underlying problem is capital and I was wondering if *Old Barn* might consider a loan—on a business basis of course—which would enable him to pay off the mortgage and finish building the studio, because it's the mortgage payments which are the killer. He needs about £2,500 to pay off the building society and then maybe a couple of hundred to cover other bills. I wouldn't ask if it wasn't a very last resort.'

Claude nodded, 'Of course, I'll ask. As you know, she's just helped me buy this place, but £2,700 might be manageable. At the end of the day I can only ask, but I'll write to her today.'

Marjorie beamed. 'Thank you *so* much. Even if it comes to nothing, I couldn't have lived with myself if we hadn't explored every avenue.'

It had become a rather sombre little party and after a few moments Marjorie said, 'Roland really wanted to come today, but he didn't dare leave the residential home because Matron has been acting so strangely and we've actually got someone from the management committee coming down today to give her notice. A man called Colonel Stewart is going to do the dreadful deed and we've been rather worried about how she might react, so I was quite relieved to be making myself scarce. It really is the *last* thing we've needed after all that's been going on with Tristan, but apart from that the Home has been going terribly well and the residents are so sweet.'

Claude leapt to his feet. 'Come and look at my cows! I can't tell you what a remedial effect they have on me, so lets hope they do the same for you.'

'There's an offer you can't refuse!' declared Josephine, laughing, before adding irresistibly, 'And if you survive *that*, then you can come and look around the house and have some lunch.'

And so the trio spread out around *Dobbler's Den* and by the time the cows had worked their restorative magic, Marjorie was feeling quite hopeful for the first time in months.

Chapter 12

July-September 1976
London
The penultimate session of group therapy had probably gone as well as Murray could have expected, although he couldn't shift a nagging disappointment that people weren't happier for him. He supposed that it was inevitable—what with human nature being inclined either to envy or outright resentment regarding the good fortune of others—but nevertheless he craved an electric reaction in even just *one* other person which would enable him to light up all over again.

Dennis—fresh from a severe bout of bronchitis—had maintained sufficiently tight discipline for no one to ridicule Murray's announcement, but for all that his news had received a very muted response and the replies from his family were similarly unsatisfactory. Although they'd been reasonably polite, the congratulations were non-existent and wishing him every happiness didn't count for much when there was no acknowledgement of the *harm* they'd done him, let alone any answers to the charges carefully spelled out in his letter.

And as if all *that* wasn't enough, he was having his own problems in sustaining the wonder and glory of it all. How *could* he sustain it, living in a council flat and only just getting by on a meagre wage? Desperately he read and re-read the Alers Hankey book he'd created until he knew it by heart, but that, too, lost its magic after the umpteenth read.

Disillusioned, he stopped taking his medication because now that his group therapy was over the shoplifting charge would be dropped and that was that.

He wished that he had more people to write to and sometimes took out his embossed, water-marked writing paper just to admire it and repeatedly read his name printed with its proper title, but the only people he had left now were Tristan and Evie. It was unfortunate that Miriam had been proved beyond any doubt to be an imposter, but quite apart from that, her unbelievably hostile behaviour towards him the previous summer had put paid to any possibility of a future relationship.

He hadn't received any news from his 'fake' family for a long time now and felt a little bereft, given that he had no contact with his *real* family either. Still, he had Frank, and now that his book was finished and there was no longer any need to go to the library, he honestly didn't know what he'd have done without that twice weekly retreat to Hove.

Together he and Frank drove all over the south coast, visiting Worthing, Southsea and all sorts of quaint little places, although by far Frank's favourite destination was Brighton. There was something about the vibrancy of the place which struck a chord with him and they spent hours on the pier, gazing out to sea and sharing successive packets of chips liberally embellished with salt and vinegar.

Murray had frequently been thankful that his courier job was sufficiently flexible to allow him so much freedom and it therefore came as a huge blow when towards the end of July his manager told him that the company was cutting back and that having been the last in, he would unfortunately be the first out. He was as nice as he could be in the circumstances and said that if the situation changed then they'd get in touch again, but for the moment they couldn't pay him beyond mid-August.

The prospect of job hunting brought back to Murray the accumulated injustices of being cut out of the Alers Hankey fortune, the disappearing fortune of *Old Barn* which should also have been his and of his situation in general. He had *some* money in the bank but that wouldn't last long and what else was there in his life? Just the dole and a council flat. Moreover, the goons were back and he'd seen the doppelganger several times—both signs that he was never going to be allowed to get on with his life. Accordingly, he changed his routes and was careful of what he said and where. It was a pain in the neck, but what else could he do?

It wasn't something he ever mentioned to Frank because the difficulties involved in getting the message across just didn't bear thinking about. And he even tried to be orderly about things: he braved the dole queues to sign on again, registered with the *Job Centre*, bought the *London Standard* to peruse the jobs and also looked through the free papers, but his heart wasn't in it. It was like a big, black hole of *déjà vu* in which he was counting time, but with no idea of what lay beyond the abyss—if anything.

Then something happened which threw him into complete disarray. He was looking through the *London Standard* as he habitually did these days, when the name *Alers Hankey* leapt out at him. It wasn't even on the front page, thank God, but hidden somewhere in the middle, with the headline, 'Duke guilty of £50,000 fraud'. Feverishly he started reading, but the words danced on the page and he repeatedly had to stop in order to calm himself.

Several attempts later and he was finally availed of the main facts:

His half-brother, the 7th Duke, had been a partner in a French-based holiday company and over time had been drawing cheques on money he wasn't entitled to in order to prop up a lavish lifestyle.

It had only been discovered when the company got into cash flow difficulties and went into receivership.

Sentencing had been adjourned, but a jail sentence was inevitable.

Murray felt the shame of this slur on his family name like a hammer blow. His old family title being dragged through the mud by an imposter who despite all his privileges had behaved like a common criminal! And there was the additional, cruel irony of this dreadful event having occurred only a couple of months or so after he'd finally discovered his connection to that noble family. Had he only known earlier, he might have enjoyed *years* of basking in the reflected glory of his ancestry, but *now*...it was irrevocably tarnished.

And that wasn't the only irony of this coincidental discovery. Had he not lost his job then he'd never have been reading the paper and would probably never have known about this blemish on the family name. It was as though fate was making a mockery of his every attempt to overcome the blows raining down on him.

No doubt his *fake* family would gloat—they almost certainly read the papers—although his group therapy partners wouldn't find out as none of them would be caught dead reading a newspaper. However, that was little consolation and having lost almost everything he valued, Murray even found himself wishing that he could go to jail instead of the 7th Duke. It was the idea of not having to worry about life anymore, but just existing to someone else's tune. Being coordinated and controlled by the prison system would certainly be easier than real life.

He felt so ashamed that he didn't even want to tell Frank and in fact didn't want to tell *anyone* because that would only reinforce how real it was. And almost more than anything else he wished that he didn't have to think about it. Overwhelmed on all counts, he simply stopped doing everything and didn't even go out except for food.

* * * * * * *

Dobbler's Den, Fivehead, Somerset

Josephine settled herself down on the sofa to re-read Marjorie's letter, which thankfully was very upbeat, although not without a heady account of misadventure.

My darlings,

I can't tell you how grateful we are to Old Barn for her wonderfully kind offer. It will make the difference between Triss managing or not managing, because lack of capital has been at the root of all his business and associated woes. He's already got someone in to help finish the studio and will start to try re-building his life, although he and Kathleen remain separated for now. At least the medication is back on track and we've all breathed a sigh of relief. He should be in a position to start making re-payments from next month but will be writing to Old Barn himself about that, and to thank her, of course.

And now I must tell you about the other adventures we've had here! You remember I told you that Matron was to be given notice by the Committee Chairman on the day I was with you? Well, would you believe that there was some last-minute delay and in the end it happened the following day when I was there after all, although in the event it was quite lucky that I was!

Well, Colonel Stewart and a welfare officer came and gave Matron notice as planned and she was naturally a little taken aback, but it all went off quite quietly to our great relief. However, shortly after they'd left the house, Roland happened to meet Matron in the passage way and she said, 'I've taken something, I'll be dead by tonight.' So Roland said, 'Don't be silly, Matron, go into your sitting room,' and then dashed into the office where I was working and told me to ring the Police.

Then suddenly the carpenter who was there doing some work for us rushed in and said that he'd seen Matron running out of the doorway and down the road and was something wrong?!

So, he and Roland raced out to our car and chased after her, eventually catching up with her quite some way down the lane. Naturally she refused to get in, so Roland and the carpenter had to force her into it, struggling and screaming, then once back here they put her into a downstairs room and Roland stationed one of the staff outside to keep an eye on her.

Meanwhile, I was desperately trying to get hold of the doctor who for some reason had gone to Norwich, so I was ringing round for another one when someone else rushed in to say that Matron had escaped again, so this time Roland and several others gave chase and saw her disappear into a bungalow at the top of the hill. She simply rushed inside when the owner answered the door and locked herself in the loo!

So Roland put the owner on guard and ran back here to tell me to call the Police again—given that no one had yet turned up—and was just about to go back to the bungalow when a member of staff ran up and said that Matron had torn down a locked door, escaped into the garden and was last seen running across fields!

By this time, Police, dogs, doctor and ambulance had all arrived and gave chase and at last managed to corner her and took her off to some mental health facility near Norwich, where last I heard she was drinking strong coffee and being comforted by staff!

We now find out that before she came to us she'd had a nervous breakdown and all that happened here had also happened at her last place up in Scotland. Would you believe it? This of course explains her extraordinary behaviour and all the various things that we've had to suffer since she arrived last January.

Poor Roland suffered from delayed shock afterwards and was really quite ill, but fortunately Matron's replacement, Sister Carter, is splendid and has already achieved more in five days than the other did in all the time she was here. Most important of all, the patients are so happy and are our great reward for all the effort we put in. They're forever telling us how comfortable they are, how good the food is, etc. etc. so we can't ask for more than that.

So, you can see that what with one thing and another we've scarcely had time to breathe, but with Tristan now hopefully back on the straight and narrow and Sister Carter running the shop here, I'm hoping that life will settle down again.

Isn't it strange how all these calamities come at once, build up to a crescendo on several fronts and then quietly melt away again, more or less at the same time?

Roland and I replied to the 'Duke' in the terms we agreed on and have heard nothing back as yet. I do so hope that things will settle down for him now.

Thank you so much again for your help in enlisting the loan from Old Barn, for which we're eternally grateful.

Etc. etc.

It seemed that one by one, the turbulent chapters of the family thriller were being closed one by one.

* * * * * * *

Murray had made a decision. It was five weeks since he'd read the fateful news article which had destroyed his life and he'd never experienced anything quite like the black desolation which followed. Since then, he'd only left the flat occasionally to get food and judging by the loose fit of his clothes had lost quite a lot of weight.

Inevitably he'd thought a lot about Frank but couldn't summon up the energy to go down to Hove, resulting in guilt being added to the melting pot of emotions which were already churning him up. However, today was different. It had been coming for a few days now, but this morning he'd woken up and his mind was clear. He felt quite calm, even content, and the impending fate of the 7th Duke of Hampshire was far from his mind. Moreover, he was going to see Frank.

It took several turns of the engine to get the *Herald* going because she'd been sitting in the garage for a few weeks now. Nevertheless, it was a beautiful day and he put the hood down, hoping that Frank wouldn't be too angry with him because his abrupt absence would have been especially disconcerting in view of the profusion of visits immediately preceding it—not to mention his promise never to abandon his brother again after the Australian trip.

He told himself that it wasn't *his* fault that Frank had no one else but him. It wasn't fair that Murray should shoulder *all* the responsibility, but given that he *did* have all the responsibility, he'd see it through to the end.

Frank was sulky. 'You didn't come,' he accused, from the refuge of the bed to which he'd taken quite soon after Murray's visits had stopped, according to a member of staff.

'I've been ill, too ill to drive, Frank, but I'm sorry and I promise that it will never happen again.'

Frank scowled. 'You promised before and you broke it.'

Murray took his hand. 'This time, I *cross my heart and hope to die*, promise.'

Frank smiled. 'All right then.'

Murray hugged him and told him not to forget his toy cars, then they left *Marlow Place*, hand in hand.

'Where first?' Murray asked, as they climbed into the car.

'Brighton.'

That was easy. He put *Wish You Were Here* into the tape deck and they drove the two miles to Brighton along the sea front, parking near the pier as usual and strolling along its length. At one point they sat down and Murray felt positively happy for the first time in as long as he could remember. He held Frank's hand, felt the wind in his hair and smelled the salt coming off the sea.

The gulls hovered hopefully but there were no chips today—or at least, not yet—and disappointed they moved on, driven ever onward by the triumph of hope over experience.

Now that school holidays and the tourist season was over, there was hardly anyone on the pier that day and it was very quiet. Similarly, Frank and Murray were also quiet because neither had done anything at all of note over the last few weeks and a peaceful silence reigned.

Murray hadn't even told Frank about losing his job, given that Frank had no interest at all in the concepts of work or money, let alone the connection between them.

Feeling that it was getting near to the time, he led Frank back to the car without saying where they were going and Frank didn't ask, then an hour later they parked on the large, green promenade at Beachy Head, facing the sea. Somewhere below in the sea was the red and white lighthouse, but it was currently hidden from them by the formidable height of the cliffs in between.

'You remember that you said you'd like to fly off this cliff…?' said Murray.

Frank looked at him, but didn't say anything.

'Well, shall we do it today? Drive really fast off the edge and for a few seconds we'll fly like a bird.'

'And then what?'

'Then we'll die.'

'Will we always be together, then?'

'Yes.'

Until then, Murray had been feeling all right, but at that point he nearly lost his nerve and it was only Frank's eyes—shining with excitement—which kept him on the level.

He turned up *Wish You Were Here* until it was blasting out at full volume, then put his foot down and the little *Herald* screeched along the short distance to the cliff edge, so that they flew over it ridiculously fast in a rush of warm air and sea salt, knocking the flimsy barrier flying.

For a few seconds the car seemed to float as if caught on an air current and in those precious moments Murray released the gearstick and grabbed Frank's hand. 'This is it! This is it!' he cried ecstatically.

Then the car started somersaulting and there was just enough time to be relieved that they were both wearing seatbelts before everything stopped.

The End

Printed in Great Britain
by Amazon

56981053R00076